Capo Dei Capi's Daughter

THE BOTTICELLI BROTHERHOOD SERIES

J.L. QUICK

CAPO DEI CAPI'S DAUGHTER COPYRIGHT
© 2023 by J.L. Quick Books LLC

All rights reserved. Printed in the United States of America. No part of this book may be used or reproduced in any manner whatsoever without the written permission except in the case of brief quotations embodied in critical articles or reviews.

This book is a work of fiction. Names, characters, businesses, organizations, places, events and incidents either are the product of the author's imagination or are used fictitiously. Any resemblance to actual persons, living or dead, events, or locales is entirely coincidental.

Cover Design: J.L. Quick

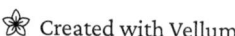 Created with Vellum

*To all the ladies whose panties get
wet when they hear these four little words...*

"Beg me to come."

Author's Note

This novel is a contemporary mafia dark romance. It contains scenes and descriptive adult content that might be triggering for some readers.

Please ensure you read the trigger warnings prior to beginning this novel.

Trigger Warnings

Criminal Activity
Death
Gun Violence
Profanity
Amaurophilia
Edging/Orgasm Control
Breeding
Masturbation
Sitophilia
Graphic Sexual Scenes
Exhibitionism
Katoptronophilia
Degradation
Anilingus
Pregnancy

Chapter One

"FUCK..."

"Yes..."

"Right there..."

"Oh my god, just like tha-"

His free hand clamps over my mouth silencing my screams.

"Shhh, cuore mio," the words a deep whisper in my ear, "I love to make you scream for me, but someone will hear us."

His words tell me to be quiet, but the relentless thrusts of his cock repeatedly slamming me against the wall tell me he wants someone to find us.

VENECIA

Shit has been tense as hell around this house for weeks. More than anything I just want to get out of here for a few hours, and spend some time with people not sulking, committing felonies, or plotting murders.

Needless to say, I was beyond excited when Chad, the captain of my college's lacrosse team, sent me a text earlier this evening. We have been texting each other for a couple of weeks now, getting to know each other a bit more than we have in the few courses we've shared. We've been out on dates a handful of times. Tonight, he wanted to get together to go out for drinks with a few of our friends.

"I think I'm gonna do it," Jessica's face drops as the words pass from my mouth.

"You mean, Princess V is finally going to lose her V-card?"

"Shhhh," I fling my hand over her face to shut her loud mouth up, "The last thing I need is for someone to hear you."

The only reason I am a twenty-two-year-old virgin is because of my family. There is no bigger cock-blocker than guys knowing your dad, brothers, cousins, and their friends will happily put a bullet in their head for laying a finger on me.

Let alone what happened to the last guy they found out tried to put one inside of me. Unfortunately for us both, he had no idea what he was doing and didn't actually make it very far. After Renzo was done with him, chances are good that he probably won't get the opportunity to figure it out either.

Being the only girl in this family can be a burden, but it also comes with perks. I am the princess. People do not tell me no. I get what I want, when I want it – except for sex apparently. When it comes to orgasms, I am completely on my own.

While I don't have anything to compare it to, I take care of the job pretty efficiently.

Unlike most guys, Chad is more than willing. He's always been handsy and has never been shy about how badly he wants to fuck me. He either is oblivious to my family or does not care.

Considering it's Chad, he's probably fucking oblivious.

After a few drinks between the two of us, we briefly made out in the back of the car on the way back to my house. His friends cheering us on from the front seat kind of ruined it for me.

They were supposed to be dropping me off, but somehow Jess and a couple of his friends wound up hanging out in my living room. As the night went on, most of them left. At this point all that's left are Chad, Jessica, and Chad's teammate, Brett, that is asleep on the couch.

I think Jessica had different plans for Brett until he threw up in the bushes and subsequently passed out.

While Chad hasn't been able to keep his hands off me all night, things definitely amplified after the car ride back to the house. As his friends have dwindled out and the night went on, his hands have been all over my hips and thighs. Occasionally I feel his fingers brush over the silk of my panties, and I am dying for him to go further.

"Jess," I grab her hand and pull her from the bathroom, "we better get back to the living room, before Papa kicks him out."

As soon as we walk back into the living room, Chad immediately pulls me back onto his lap and presses his hand between my thighs. His hand slides up my thigh as he begins to whisper in my ear, "Let's go somewhere we can be alone. I want to see if you can own up to all the shit you've been talking all night. I want to see you on your knees sucking my fucking cock."

"That's funny," I whisper back as he kisses along my neck, "I was thinking about letting you finally show me."

"Show you what, beautiful?"

"Everything you've been saying I'm missing out on, by not letting you fuck me."

"Fuck sucking my cock, I'd much rather pop your...," his words cut short when he is distracted by Lorenzo at the bar.

He is a mess. His hair is disheveled, and he has blood splattered across his white shirt. This is the way I have seen Renzo most of my life. It's who he is. I love my brother, regardless of the fact that he is a sociopath.

For someone who didn't seem to give a fuck about my family five minutes ago, Chad looks as though he has seen a ghost. It is as though he had the sudden realization that every rumor he has heard about my brothers might actually be true, and he can't seem to get his hands off me fast enough.

And the Botticelli Brotherhood cock-block strikes again.

"It's late. Get one of the guys to take your friends home," Renzo commands after a few minutes of not-so-pleasantries. I know it's not up for debate. They can go or he can make them go.

After quick and uncomfortable goodbyes, I head upstairs to my room to yet another lonely night with my vibrator.

Chapter Two

VENECIA

Yet another text to Chad left unread. It's been days without a word from him, so I guess I can officially count him out.

Heading downstairs, I am caught off guard by my father and a guy I have never seen before. I would definitely remember having seen him around the house before.

He is tall, definitely a little over six feet. He looks older, maybe in his mid- to late-thirties, but based on how broad and muscular he is, he's probably in better shape than most guys my age. While his build is too big for it, his face looks like it could belong to a model. Especially with that slicked back, jet-black hair and that rugged jaw line, which is currently carrying just the right amount of several days of scruff. But what really stands out about him is those smoldering green eyes.

Calm yourself, V…

Based on his expensive suit and ridiculous muscular build, he obviously works for the family. I could look at him all I want, but there isn't a man that works for my father that would even think about putting a hand on me. Hell, most of them barely manage to make eye contact with me out of fear.

"V…Princess," my father calls when he sees me, "I was going to introduce the two of you later at dinner, but since you are here."

I nervously tuck the tendril of my messy bun behind my ear as I walk towards them. Had I known I was going to be meeting someone this morning, especially this man, I would have preferred to have taken a moment to make myself a tad more presentable.

"V, this is Dante DeLuca," my father says as he reaches out his hand to shake mine. I reach back and his massive hand engulfs mine as he gently shakes it.

"Nice to meet you Miss Venecia," his deep voice vibrates as he speaks, "Please just call me Dante. I hope to not be too much of an inconvenience for you."

"I'm sorry?" I let go of his hand and look towards my father questioningly.

"With everything going on, I refuse to leave you unprotected. You aren't like your brothers. You aren't prepared to take care of yourself if it becomes necessary. And I will not let anything happen to my little princess."

"So, Dante…"

"He will be driving you anytime you leave the house. Beyond that, he is good at his job, and you will barely notice he is around," my father responds,

"Essentially, he is going to be your bodyguard."

"You've got to be kidding me," I huff, as I eye him up and down.

Great. Now I have a babysitter.

If I'm going to be stuck with him, I am going to make this as unpleasant for him as possible, "We're going out tonight at ten. So, I suggest you rest up, old man."

A smug smile tugs at the corner of his mouth.

Turning to head back upstairs, I overhear my father informing Dante that I can be a bit of a handful.

I intend to be way more than a handful. This fucker isn't going to stick around, regardless of how nice he might be to look at.

I do not need yet another man following me around and ensuring I don't do anything they hypocritically deem to be inappropriate. Seriously, Renzo is fucking some girl he bought – and we're almost the same age. And while I never see him with anyone, I'm certain that Carlo is getting plenty as well.

Pulling out my phone I send out a bunch of texts letting everyone know the plans for tonight. There is a rave happening at an old warehouse down by the docks. Shortly after texts go out, Jessica is texting back as to what time to come over and get ready.

Since my babysitter seemed to be everywhere that I tried to go in and around the house today, I wound up spending most of the day alone in my room. When Jessica knocks on my door, I am excited to finally have someone to talk to.

"Who's the DILF in the living room," she questions as soon as she lets herself in.

"That's Dante," I sigh, "Apparently Papa doesn't think I'm capable of being out in public on my own. So, he hired him to babysit me."

"Fuck," Jessica licks her lips, "he can babysit me. Maybe if I act up, he'll spank me."

"Do you ever think about anything else?"

"No, I don't. Do you?"

I roll my eyes and turn back to my closet, mostly out of annoyance that she is right. I spend a lot of time thinking about something I technically know absolutely nothing about.

Digging through the clothes in my closet, I finally find the black leather mini skirt I was looking for and change into it. Continuing to scour my closet, I grab a black lacy cropped camisole.

"Damn, V," Jessica looks me over, "If you are trying to make Chad jealous or find someone new, that is definitely the outfit to do it."

Taking a look at myself in the mirror, she isn't wrong. I was naturally blessed with a body that would make most girls jealous – I am tall, lean, and curvy in all the right places. The clothes I put on only accentuate all those features.

Grabbing a brush, I pull my straight black hair into a sleek high ponytail. After making a quick update to darken my lipstick and freshen up my cat-eye, I am ready to go.

Chapter Three

DANTE

Babysitting the boss's daughter was not exactly what I had in mind when Sal approached me about needed to talk to me about a special job.

I expected him to use my...skills...for something more in line with the work that Lorenzo and Luca do for the family.

That said, Sal also is not the type of boss that you say no to. At least not if you want to continue to be able to speak.

While I had never met her before, I have heard stories about Venecia. Most of them just ramblings of guys working for the family, talking about how wild and crazy she is or the risqué nights they had sneaking around with the Capo Dei Capi's daughter.

Having heard Sal talk about his daughter before, and observing just how protective he was of her, I had always just figured it was all locker room talk and nothing but a bunch of bullshit. There isn't a man in this city that would be lucky enough to walk away from her with his hands, let alone his life.

After meeting her today though, I am no longer certain. She doesn't come across as a demure, sheltered, mafia princess. One thing is for sure, she is more beautiful than a single guy had ever described her to be. A beauty like hers naturally draws attention, and it is going to be difficult to keep men away from her. It is going to be difficult to keep her safe.

Hearing heels clicking down the stairs, I stand from the couch to meet Venecia in the hallway. A quiet growl rises in my chest as I take her in. She was beautiful when I saw her all fresh out of bed and disheveled earlier, but she is fucking enticing as hell right now. The black heels and mini skirt show off her long, tanned, and toned legs. Her cleavage spills in a modestly perfect amount from the top of her shirt, while exposing her waist and a tiny tattoo over her belly button. A sleek black ponytail rests of her right shoulder. The way her hair is pulled back shows of the features of her face and her long, slender neck.

Fuck other men. It's going to be difficult to keep myself away from her.

This is the boss's kid, emphasis on kid, and all I can think about right this second, is wrapping those long legs around my head and what she may or may not have on underneath that tiny skirt.

Definitely a strappy little thong. Fuck! Get your shit together, Dante!

Heading to the door, I open it for the two of them, "I pulled the Tahoe around front. Are we picking up anyone else on the way?"

"No. It's just us.," Venecia says flatly as she walks down the stairs and climbs into the back of the SUV.

The girls have requested that the music playing be turned up, leaving me unable to listen in on the conversation happening in the backseat as we drive towards the docks.

Pulling up to the warehouse, I come to a stop as someone steps in front of the Tahoe. My head spins around to the backseat when I notice that the sounds of outside suddenly become significantly louder.

"Thanks, Dante," Jessica and Venecia have the rear door open and are sliding out of the backseat, "we'll get out here."

"Wait," I call back as they both shut their doors and scurry into the warehouse.

Fuck! Apparently she really is a handful.

Blaring the horn to get people out of my way, I pull around the side of the building, quickly park the Tahoe and make my way to the entrance.

"Where do you think you're going," the large bouncer puts his hand against my chest when I try to walk past him, "Line is around the corner."

"I'm with the girl that just went in. Black mini skirt and a long black ponytail."

His bear claw of a hand gently pushes me back urging me to walk towards the line, "There's no way you are with that gorgeous fucking girl."

"Would you believe I have a ten-inch cock and fuck like a porn star?"

"You're funny man."

"I got one more for you," I step closer to him and lower my voice, "Would you believe she's Salvatore Botticelli's daughter and if anything happens to her because I'm not in there that you'll be a fucking dead man by sunrise."

Stepping out of the way, he gestures for me to pass, "Um, yeah, go on in."

Once inside, I quickly begin scanning the massive crowd. There are hundreds of people crammed into this warehouse. Some are dancing in groups; others are lingering in the dark partaking in illicit activities or substances along the outskirts of the party.

My eyes continue scouring through the faces in the crowd searching for Venecia, who I finally spot dancing in the center of improvised dance floor. Keeping my eyes fixated on her, I work my way through the crowd until I reach the bar located at the back of building.

"Club soda with lime," I drop ten dollars on the counter. The bartender looks at me as though he has never served a non-alcoholic drink before, but promptly passes me my order. Taking it from him, I walk towards one of the support beams nearby. Leaning with my back against it, I sip my drink and continue to keep my eyes on her.

Realistically, it would be hard to pull my eyes from her. If not impossible.

As if she didn't garner enough attention from her sheer appearance, she is amazing to watch on the dance floor. Her body sways and bounces to the music, her hands roaming her body as she moves. Unlike most of the other women dancing, she isn't trying to be sexy or entice men to her. In contrast, she is oblivious to everyone around her, every ounce of sensuality she exudes in this moment is for her.

I watch two guys slowly approach her through the crowd. They look like two predators inching towards wounded prey, causing my jaw to clench while my fingers flex around my glass. I drop my glass to the ground, and my eyes dart between the hunters and

Venecia as I quickly make my way through the crowd.

She never sees them coming. They slink around her, boxing her between them as they place their hands on her body and begin to grind their bodies against her. While she has a smile on her face and continues dancing, the look in her eyes and her body language has changed dramatically. She no longer looks free and uninhibited. Instead, she looks as though she is trying to hide the fact that she feels as though she is boxed in as she tries to get a little distance from their bodies and wandering hands.

Pressing through the last of the crowd, I reach them as the one grinding behind her attempts to lift her skirt.

Chapter Four

VENECIA

Small beads of sweat trickle down my back and between my breasts as I dance. This is my therapy. Pouring the emotions from my body, I can let go. I don't have to be anything for anyone. I can clear my mind.

I don't go out to party and get drunk or high. This feeling of freedom is more than enough of a high for me.

It never fails that some handsy jerk needs to ruin it for me. I am pulled from my happy bliss when I feel a pair of hands grab my hips, promptly followed by them roughly pulling me back against his body. Continuing to dance, I try to make a little space between us but am stopped as another man steps in front of me. His icy fingers wrap around my waist as he steps towards me, sandwiching me tightly between the two of them.

Plastering a smile on my face, I continue to dance as they grind against me. My hands on theirs, in an unfruitful attempt to keep them in places I am semi-comfortable with. A very unsuccessful attempt, as the guy grinding his erection against my ass begins to lift my skirt.

My hands are fumbling for his, trying to keep him from pulling it over my ass when he suddenly stops and both men take a small step back from me.

"There you are baby. I thought I told you not to wander off," Dante's deep voice billows over the music as his hand grips my jaw and pulls my face up towards his. Fully expecting him to stop, I am completely shocked when he pulls my face against his lips.

His warm, soft, full lips...

A soft, gentle kiss. Both our lips are slightly parted, and I can taste the citrus from his drink as he sucks my lower lip into his mouth. My heart is thumping in my chest when he lets go of my chin. Pulling his face back, our eyes meet for a searing second. Our gazes only broken because he spins me around.

Wrapping his hands around my waist, he pulls me against him. The firm body pressed against me feels comforting and I melt into him. Goosebumps run down my neck as his lips brush against my ear and he whispers, "You're okay. I've got you."

His chest against my back and my head resting just against his shoulder, his hands hold my hips. Using them, he moves my hips with his to the beat of the music pounding around us.

Unlike most men, he isn't grinding his dick against my ass as he dances with me to try to get himself off. His movements are slow and sensual, as though he is savoring every second of holding me and how he can move my body.

I can't get enough...

Heavy breaths continue to escape my mouth, a combination of exertion and what his hands on my skin are doing to my body. With one hand against my stomach continuing to guide my body, the other slides up the curves of my side and over my shoulder until his fingers delicately wrap around my throat.

With his hands wrapped around my body we continue to move together to the music as though our bodies are one. My pulse is racing, my panties are soaked, and my body is on fucking fire from this man holding me against his body. A man I swore only a few hours ago to drive away.

The way he holds me and touches me it feels like it has purpose...confidence. Confidence that I have not yet come across with the guys I meet that are my own age.

The hand around my throat tips my head to the side and pulls it back against his shoulder. My lips tremble as I feel his warm breath move from the nape of my neck towards my ear. Those soft lips graze over my earlobe, before stopping against my ear.

"Those guys are gone," his deep voice trembles through me, "you don't have to worry about them anymore."

He turns me around, still holding me tight to his body as he stares down into my eyes.

"Are you good," he questions in the upmost professional tone.

Nodding my head at him, his hands slide from my body.

"I'll be over at the bar," he gestures his head towards the bar, "if you need anything. And if anything goes wrong, I will be right here for you."

He steps away from me and within seconds he is swallowed by the crowd. My body stands motionless amongst this sea of people, as he disappears, and I no longer feel the warmth of his body against me.

Feeling a body bump into me, I turn to find Jessica.

"You okay," she questions as she begins to dance against me, "you look like something is off."

Awkwardly beginning to dance again I respond to her. "Um...yeah," I lie, "Those guys just creeped me out."

"What guys?"

Chapter Five

DANTE

Fuck!

Adjusting my semi-hard cock, I keep my eyes on Venecia as I walk back to the bar. Dropping a twenty-dollar bill on the counter to get the bartender's attention, I order a double of bourbon. As he grabs the bottle from the shelf, I change my order to a club soda. As much as I need it to take the edge off, I am still on the job.

Fuck, the job.

The interaction on the dance floor was not what I had walked over there for. My intention was to intimidate the two guys bothering her without making a scene.

I just couldn't stop myself from kissing her.

Holding her against me and dancing wasn't necessary. Those two left as soon as I loomed over them, but I wanted to feel her.

I wanted to hold her body against me to see what she felt like, and I couldn't stop myself.

What the fuck am I doing?

She's the boss's daughter; he'd fucking kill me just for thinking about laying a hand on her.

She's a child for Christ's sake.

Okay, she's not a child, but I am old enough to almost be her father.

Standing near the bar, I nurse glass after glass of club soda while keeping a keen eye on Venecia. Her friend disappeared with some guy a few hours ago, but she stayed on the dance floor enjoying herself. The hours have passed by and there are significantly less people here than when we arrived. It is nearly four in the morning when she stops dancing and begins to make her way to the bar. More correctly, she begins to make her way to me.

"Ready to head home, Miss Venecia," I shout over the music as she approaches me.

She scrunches her nose as she nods back to me. Following a few steps behind her, she leads me through the building and back out to the parking lot.

She stops when she realizes she doesn't know where the car is.

"Over this way," I gesture around the corner of the building.

Venecia walks by my side in silence the rest of the way to the car. As we approach, I press the key fob in my pocket to unlock the doors. Reaching the SUV, I step in front of her to open the rear door. The gentlemanly notion of offering my hand to help her in is quickly shoved from my mind, as I do not trust myself to touch her again.

"Seatbelt," I command as I slide myself into the driver's seat and fasten my own. Looking into the rearview, I watch as she presses a gentle huff over her pouty lips before reaching for the belt.

Not a word is spoken on the way back to the Botticelli estate. On occasion, I would look into the rearview mirror to find her piercing blue eyes staring inquisitively at me. Something was on her mind and words were sitting at the tip of her tongue, but whenever my eyes met hers in the mirror her gaze would divert to the floor or out the window.

Pulling through the gate and heading up the long drive, I am hoping that tonight's events can be successfully passed off to Sal as trying to keep her protection discreet. If not, I am so fucked.

From here on out, be a professional Dante. As if your life depends upon it...because it fucking does.

Reaching the stairs to the estate, I put the SUV in park and quickly exit to open Venecia's door. This time I offer her my hand to aid in her exit. She averts her gaze from me and pushes past my hand as she slides out of the SUV.

Turning her head back to me, a sinister smile spreads across her face, "You do know what Papa does to guys that put their hands on me, right?"

I am so fucked...

Chapter Six

DANTE

As quickly as she snarked out those words, she turns and walks up the stairs into the house. Meanwhile, I am left standing by the SUV, wondering how much longer I have to live. Climbing back into the SUV, I drive it over to the garage before heading inside to meet my fate.

Walking up the front steps and into the house, my eyes are drawn to the far end of the front hall. Venecia is hugging Sal at the bottom of the steps.

"Good night, Papa," she says, giving him a kiss on the cheek. Shooting a wicked smirk at me, she turns and heads upstairs.

"Dante," Sal's deep voice billows through the hallway when he sees me standing at the front door, "I need to see you in my office."

Fuuuuuck...

Each step down this long hallway feels like I am slowly walking towards my own execution. My last meal having been a club soda and lime.

Yet another shitty life decision.

By the time I traverse the hallway and turn into Sal's office, he is already seated behind his desk. His position in this office makes it quite clear that he is the one who holds all of the power in this situation.

"Shut the door," he waves his hand towards me as soon as my foot crosses the threshold.

Immediately doing as I am told; I turn and gently close the door behind me. Quietly, I let out a deep breath before turning and walking towards Sal.

"Sit," he demands when I approach the desk.

Settling into one of the upholstered chairs opposite of Sal, I unsuccessfully attempt to discern the current look on his face. I feel my heart rate increase as he stares at me and begins to drum his fingers on the desk.

If he is trying to torture me with silence, he is actually being quite successful.

"So," he takes a long drawn out pause to take a sip of his drink, "V informed me that there was an issue this evening."

His extended silence is my cue that he is awaiting my response.

"Yes," I gulp, "I apologize, sir. Things got out of hand this evening."

He continues to stare me down as though Venecia didn't already tell him everything that happened this evening. As though he doesn't already know that I had my lips on hers, my hands all over her and that he is just waiting for me to confess it to him.

"There were two guys who were getting a little too close to Venecia. It was obvious that she was uncomfortable in their presence," I pause to carefully choose my next words, "I was trying to resolve the situation without drawing attention."

Just as I am about to continue with my confession, Sal stands from behind his desk.

"I appreciate your discretion, Dante," his words shock me as he walks around the desk, "and so does V."

After using my hand to physically verify that my mouth isn't agape, I simply stare at Sal in utter confusion.

"Most guys would have come out guns blazing or throwing fists. While she knows what we do as a family and she is not ashamed of us, she does prefer to try to live as normal of a life as possible. Discretion in watching over her is quite important. I am quite pleased to see that you understood that without being implicitly told."

Sal leans forward and his large hand firmly grips my shoulder before he continues, "After tonight, I know that I have chosen the right man for this job."

Still at a complete loss for words, I force a smile onto my face before nodding at him appreciatively.

Little does he know; I am appreciative that I still have both my hands...and my heart is still beating.

"This is an ask, not a tell," Sal leans back so that he is resting against the desk, "I would like for you to stay here. There is obviously plenty of room for you."

Reaching behind him onto the desk, he picks up his drink and takes another long sip.

"I love my daughter," he chuckles, "but she is a handful. I need you in her presence at all times. While I love her, I do not trust her to be obedient. She gets that from her mother. I need you to ensure she is not sneaking out of the house without you."

The only words I can muster sputter from my mouth,

"I understand."

"Good," his smile suddenly wide, "I will have her brothers keep an eye on her today. Although, it's probably not necessary because she will likely sleep until this afternoon. That should give you plenty of time to gather the items that you need to get situated here. In the meantime, I will have the room across from V readied for you."

Taking the hint that this is the end of our conversation, I stand from my chair and walk towards the door. Turning the handle, I am pretty sure I just got my stay of execution.

What the fuck just happened?

Chapter Seven

VENECIA

It is around two in the afternoon, when I finally decide to pull myself from bed. I would happily sleep for a few more hours, but I'm hungry and someone is making a fuck-ton of noise in the hallway. I take a second to pull my hair into a messy bun and grab a hoodie to throw on while heading downstairs.

My feet stop in their tracks when I open the door, suddenly seeing what the commotion is. And it happens to be in the room across the hall from mine.

You've got to be fucking kidding me!

Dante has a few suitcases open on the bed and he is banging around trying to find places to put his things.

"What are you doing?" I storm across the hall to the open doorway.

"Good afternoon, sleepyhead," he mumbles back at me, continuing to put his things away, "I was beginning to wonder if you were going to sleep all day".

Clutching my sweatshirt in my fist, I stomp towards him and swing it at his arm.

"Would you mind leaving my room?" his eyes glance towards me, "I'm trying to unpack my things."

"Your room?"

"Yes, Miss Venecia. My room."

"You don't have your own place," I scoff back at him.

"I do. And I like it there. It's quiet and I don't tend to get hit," a bit of annoyance tinges his voice, "But your father seems to think I need to be around all the time to keep an eye on you."

Taking a step closer to him, I lower my voice, "Do you really think that's a good idea?"

"I follow the boss's orders," his voice is flat as he turns to face me, "Why wouldn't it be a good idea?"

"You know," my voice quiet as I feel my cheeks begin to flush, "with what happened last night."

His eyes scan over my body and a look I can't quite distinguish comes over his face.

Disgust, maybe?

"I'm sorry if you got the wrong idea last night," he pauses and takes a step back from me, "but nothing happened. You're a nice kid, but I was simply doing my job. Keeping you safe and trying not to draw attention."

Standing in front of him, I suddenly feel so exposed and vulnerable. My face is on fire, the blush of my cheeks a clear tell of my current embarrassment. I sheepishly pull the oversized hoodie over my head as though covering my body is going to rid me of the embarrassment currently coursing through me. Tugging at the hem, I pull it down my body. As it covers my shorts, I shove both of my hands into the front pocket, a poor effort to hide as much of me as possible.

My eyes are still fixated on the floor, the wall, out the window – anything but Dante – as I step backwards.

"I didn't mean," I fumble for the words to continue as he returns to his belongings, "Never mind..."

Suddenly, not feeling nearly as hungry as I was a few minutes ago, I quickly turn and cross the hall back to my room. Glancing up towards Dante as I quietly shut the door, I see him fully engrossed in unpacking again. It is as though I wasn't just in the room a moment ago and he couldn't care less.

About last night or my feelings.

DANTE

Fumbling with the items in my suitcase, trying to maintain the facade of my heartless attitude, I drop them and let out a large exhale when I hear Venecia's door finally click shut.

From the moment Sal so-called suggested that I move in here, I knew it was going to be a bad idea.

Probably the worst idea...being around her 24/7.

But who am I to disobey the boss?

After our meeting, I went home to gather some of my things. As much as I desperately needed to get some sleep, I could not get all the thoughts of her out of my mind. Thoughts of my hands on her body quickly turned to my hands on my cock, gliding over my length as I continued to think about her body rubbing against mine. Even after relieving myself, my cock still ached for her. Somehow, I managed to get a little rest before I packed up a few weeks' worth of things.

Her body in my hands has barely left my mind since last night.

The entire drive back to the estate, I thought about all the reasons this wasn't going to work out. The biggest of all walked across the hall and straight into my room.

From the moment her delicate feet hit the threshold, it was a struggle to keep my eyes off her. Her long, tan legs were fully exposed with the tiny boy-shorts she was wearing. As if that weren't enough to marvel at, the gap between her shorts and shirt showed just a little of her midriff, a place I thoroughly enjoyed grazing my hand over last night. Her thin shirt was just sheer enough to distinguish the pink circles around the pert nipples pressing against the taught fabric. Her face, a beautiful mixture of anger and intrigue.

Seeing her like that, the urge to place my hands on her again is physically painful. Never in my life have I been this compelled in my need to be with a woman. Not touching her again feels like a fate worse than death.

The moment she pulled on her sweatshirt to hide her painful embarrassment, was both crushing and relieving for me.

While it vaguely helped to mitigate my urges to touch her, seeing the hurt in her eyes over my complete apathy towards her was worse than any torture I have endured in my life.

It had to be done.

She will think I am a complete asshole and have nothing but disdain for me. But that means from here on out, I can simply do my job. I will be a professional.

No wandering eyes. No wandering hands.

If only I could get her out of my head...

* * *

Things have been growing progressively tense in this house since I moved in a couple of weeks ago. Thankfully, it is not related to me and the numerous indiscretions constantly running through my mind about the woman I am supposed to be keeping safe.

Since I lied to Venecia about that night at the club, pretending it was just work, she has pretty much been indifferent to me. Having me around seems like it is much more than an annoyance for her. She keeps her distance, ensures we never make contact, and speaks to me as little as possible.

The hatred from her over my faux apathy is excruciating. When I am in her presence, the only thing I can think about is running my hands over her skin again and pulling her close. At night, alone in my room, when my hand wraps around my cock, she is the only woman I think about. My wet palm a poor substitute for the tight little cunt I want to claim as my own, fucking her until she can't even remember another man's touch.

Chapter Eight

VENECIA

Since the day Dante moved in and I questioned that moment on the dance floor, things have just been horribly uncomfortable. Every time we wind up in the same room or confined in a car, I relive that moment of sheer embarrassment. Every day I am reminded of what a bumbling ass I made of myself.

Funny enough, the awkwardness has nothing to do with actually thinking that there was something. I've read too many of Mom's old rom coms from the library to explain it any other way, but there was definitely a spark. A connection. A fleeting moment. Something happened that night.

Whatever it was though, he has been very clear that he doesn't want anything to happen.

Hello, every other guy I've met in my life - except for Chad.

To give him what he wants, I am doing my best to keep my distance. Except when absolutely necessary, I try not to be around him. While I usually make small talk with Papa's guys who drive me around, I keep ours to the bare minimum. No pleasantries.

He's made it a point not to actually look at me. Those gorgeous green eyes look around me, even when he's speaking to me.

I want to feel them bore through my soul again.

Above all, he is extremely careful about not touching me - ever. There is always ample room for me to pass when he opens doors. He doesn't extend a hand to help me in or out of a car.

I need him to touch me again, so I can see if it was real.

Having taken three shots while at the club tonight, I'm feeling a tad more brazen than usual.

Fuck embarrassment.

There is no reason we can't be adults. No reason we can't talk about this and clear the air.

"Dante," the sound of his name breaking the silence in this car is almost deafening. I watch as his fingers grip the wheel a little tighter and can see a slight tick in the muscles of his jaw as he ever so slightly clenches his jaw.

"Miss," his tone is flat, respectful and professional.

"I'm not one for subtleties, so I'm just going to put this out there," I take a deep breath and word vomit everything that I've been thinking for the past couple of weeks, "I'm sorry that I brought up something that made you uncomfortable. I've kept my distance and given you space, in hopes that my embarrassment and this awkwardness would pass."

"Venecia," my name slowly draws from his mouth as though it pains him to say it.

"I'm not done," I quickly silence him, "It's not getting better. It's actually just getting worse. The more you try not to touch me or look at me, the more uncomfortable you make me feel. So, can you just stop? Can you just pretend I never said anything?"

His fingers flex around the steering wheel until his knuckles turn white as he gives a gruff, "No."

The nerve of this fucking man...

"No?" my body shifts uncomfortably in my seat, "you can't be an adult about things and just let it go? Move on?"

The fingers flexing around the steering wheel look as though they are trying to tear it in two. That little tick in his jaw is now a full clench that must be physically painful, and I can see the veins slowly bulging in his neck.

DANTE

Listening to Venecia, my fingers wrap around the steering wheel until my knuckles turn white.

Can I pretend she never said anything?

Metaphorically I bite my tongue, but physically I clench my jaw so hard I am almost unable to speak, "No."

"No," she echoes back my reply.

I can hear her fidgeting in the back and feel her eyes staring at me, "you can't be an adult about things and just let it go? Move on?"

Just let it go?

Move on?

Her words have me filled with what can only be described as rage. My jaw clenches and my fingers grip harder around the steering wheel, both physically painful. My physical pain is the only thing keeping me from inflicting more undue emotional pain on her.

"No," I bark back at her, "I am being a fucking adult about things, but no, I can't just fucking let it go and move on."

From the sound of her breathing, it is apparent that she startled at my angered response.

"Not touching you, trying to keep my eyes off you," an angry sigh expels from my lungs, "that is me being the fucking adult."

"Dante," her voice soft and hesitant.

"No, this time I'm not done," I interrupt her, "I look at you every fucking chance I get. I can barely fucking take my eyes off you. And it's not that I don't want to touch you, Venecia. It's that I fucking can't. Touching your skin, holding you against me, and feeling those pouty fucking lips against mine are the only fucking things I think about.

"Then..."

"I can't touch you," the words fueled with the ache I've been trying to hide for weeks, "I don't trust myself to touch even an inch of your perfect fucking skin and manage to restrain myself from owning every last part of your body."

"What if," she hesitates, the fear of what she intends to say trembles through her words as she speaks, "What if I said, 'I'm not stopping you?'"

The words are no sooner out of her mouth and my head is snapping around to look at her.

I have to see her face, to look into her eyes.

"What if," my eyes lock on hers and I watch as her chest heaves and her breath hitches, "if I want you as badly as you want me?"

Those words, coupled with the look in her eyes, has my heart racing. My aching cock is throbbing against my zipper with every thump of heart.

"What being pressed against your body with your hands all over me is the only thing I think about?"

My hands grip the seat backs and I lean between them as I prepare to climb into the backseat with her, "Vene-."

The car behind us obnoxiously honks their horn, simultaneously interrupting me and bringing me back to the reality I need to face.

Turning around, I notice that the car behind us is honking because the traffic light has turned green. Grabbing the steering wheel, I put my focus back on the road and accelerate through the intersection.

The uncomfortable silence has returned to the car, and I cannot bring myself to look at her. I manage only to steal a glimpse or two in the mirror.

The reality that she is off-limits, definitely for a guy like me, hits me and I let out a dismal sigh, "You know we can't."

Chapter Nine

VENECIA

It was better when I thought he hated me, and he couldn't look at me. Knowing that he can't stand to be around me because he wants me is torture.

Every fleeting glance causes my pulse to race and my mind to flood. Thoughts of him touching me and having his way with me while wondering if he's thinking the same has my panties constantly dampened with my arousal.

While I've tried to bring it up again, he promptly ends the discussion with a pained version of, "we can't."

Needing to get him out of my head, I convinced Jessica to head out to the clubs with me. In her normal fashion, she ditched me for some guy she met on the dance floor a few hours later.

It's fine though, the thumbing beat from the DJ booth has me in my own little world as I dance alone on the dance floor. I'm so checked out from all of my thoughts that I don't even notice when he sneaks up behind me and wraps his hands around my waist.

"Hello, beautiful."

Turning around, I am met with his face leaning down to kiss me. Pushing him from my body, "Are you fucking kidding me? How fucking drunk are you?"

His hands stretch out towards me, grabbing my hips and aggressively pulling me back towards his body.

"You know you missed your Daddy."

"Gross Chad," I shove him again, "you know how I feel about that shit."

"C'mon," he grabs for my arm, "you know I'm just fucking around."

From the corner of my eye, I see Dante approaching us from the bar. Putting my hand up, I signal for him to stop.

I don't need him to take care of this for me.

"You don't get to ghost me and then show back up like nothing has happened."

"I didn't ghost you beautiful," his hands roam over my arms, "Coach had me on two-a-day practices, beautiful. You know how it gets."

Shaking my head at him, I know he's full of shit, but tonight I don't care.

I do care, but fuck it.

While she might not have the soundest of advice, tonight I'm going to listen to Jessica, "The best way to get over guy is to get under another one."

"Fine…"

"The guys and I have a couch in VIP. Come hang out with us for a while," he takes my hand and begins to pull me through the crowd.

Half of the lacrosse team is on the other side of the VIP ropes. Thanks to ample bottle service, shots are flowing freely. The guys are taking them two at a time while liberally sharing them with the already drunk girls hanging all over them.

Chad pulls me onto his lap as he sits on the couch. From the view across from us, it is apparent some have already gotten their girls pliable. Hidden from most of the club thanks to the rowdy crowd of teammates, Brett and Mark are currently sharing a blonde. She is bent at the waist, her skirt hiked over her hips and her panties dangling around her ankles. Brett taking her from behind while she sucks off Mark.

Turning my attention away from them, Chad is promptly holding a shot glass to my lips. Without thinking, I down the shot.

Fucking tequila.

Pulling the glass from my lips, Chad is shoving the lime, which is between his lips, into my mouth. I've barely shaken the after-burn of the tequila and his tongue plunges into my mouth. His kiss is wet and sloppy, but not nearly as sloppy as the hand he keeps trying to run up my thigh under my skirt.

Breaking the kiss, he spills tequila all over the table preparing two more shots, before putting one in my hand. When I don't shoot right away, his hand slowly lifts the glass up to my lips encouraging me to take it.

His hands continue to grope my hips and thighs, and I can feel him growing hard underneath me. When I look at him, I am no longer certain if it's because of me or the show going on across from us.

Kyle has unzipped and is pressing his erection in front of the blonde's face. Putting Mark in her hand and pumping him, I watch as she takes Kyle into her mouth.

"How many do you think she can take," his whisper slurs in my ear, turning my stomach, as another guy approaches them and begins rubbing himself through his pants.

Turning his attention back to me, he tries to shove his hand under my shirt as I shove it away, "Do you like watching them? Does it make you wet? Do you see how well she takes all that dick?"

Even as the tequila begins to hit me, it is obvious that the words coming from him are arousing him.

I actually don't think he gives a shit how this makes me feel - Uncomfortable as fuck.

Sliding me off his lap, I watch as he undoes his zipper and pulls out his erection. He strokes it with his hand as he continues to talk, "I bet you can suck a cock way better than she can. Show me how you suck this dick."

Fucking really?

I am so caught off guard that he had the gall to say it with a horrible Paul Rudd impression, that he manages to grab the back of my head and shove it towards his dick.

"Chad," I struggle unsuccessfully to push myself back up against his hand.

"Suck Daddy's dick like a good little girl."

DANTE

I let her call me off when I tried to approach, but I cannot stand seeing him with her. Watching the way this douche of a frat boy puts his hands on Venecia makes my blood pump with rage.

I want to be the one putting my hands all over her.

I have been watching her like a hawk since she passed the velvet robes into what is obviously date rape central. My nostrils flaring and my fists clenched at my sides, I fight against myself to not cross through the ropes and beat the ever-loving shit out of him for merely thinking it's okay for him to touch her.

She continues to keep his roaming hands at bay, but watching him paw at her like she's a fucking piece a meat, a mere conquest, has me fucking seething.

Her face grows increasingly uncomfortable. Something has her on edge, but regardless of my vantage point I am unable to see what is happening in front of her.

That is obviously the point behind the wall of drunk muscle.

The moment I see him going for his zipper, my feet begin carrying me to the VIP entrance. Quickly crossing the distance to the velvet ropes, I am stopped by two guys who are definitely with the frat boy.

"Sorry, old man," one of them gently pushes me back,

"This isn't your kind of party."

Behind them, I watch as he grabs her head and forcefully shoves it toward his cock while she struggles to stop him.

Lifting my shirt and pull the gun tucked in the front of my pants, "I'm inviting myself. You can let me through, or I can make room for myself."

Both of them step aside making room for me to pass, and my fist is immediately in frat boy's face. Catching him off-guard, Venecia has an opportunity to sit up and move away from him.

"What the fuck, bro," the last words I hear from him before my fists begin unleashing every ounce of rage into his face.

"The lady fucking said 'no'," I punch him again, before grabbing his shirt and lifting his body from the couch, "maybe you didn't hear her."

"I didn't," he blubbers back through swollen and split lips as I hold him off the ground.

We've garnered the attention of the group I couldn't see from outside of the VIP – four guys with their cocks out and a nearly naked girl so drunk she can't stand on her own.

Dropping him to the ground, I grab the arm he used to shove Venecia into his crotch and yank it behind him until he is squirming in agony.

"Well," I lift it higher, "Are you going to fucking apologize?"

"I...I'm sorry...V," he sputters through the pain.

"That didn't really sound like you meant it," my hands yank his arm tighter until I feel his shoulder pop from the socket. He screams out in agony as I throw his body to the floor, leaving him writhing in pain, "besides, her brothers would be disappointed if I left you with two working hands."

Turning to the other assholes, "Did this one even say 'yes'?"

"She didn't say 'no'," the drunk guy holding her upright chodes as one of his friends sternly elbows him in the ribs.

"Are you fucking kidding me," I scowl, shoving my gun against the base of his cock.

"Bro! Bro! I was just kidding," he stammers back with wide eyes.

"Put your pathetic fucking cocks away," I tuck the gun back into my pants and pull off my shirt. Pulling the girl from their grasps, I hold her upright while pulling my shirt over her head to cover her.

"This is not how men fucking treat women. If I find any of you doing this shit again, it'll be the last time you get to pull your sad little cock out of your pants. Nod that you understand."

All of them tremble out a nod of agreement, including the frat boy crying on the floor.

"Venecia," I growl while lifting the drunk girl into my arms, "We're leaving."

Chapter Ten

VENECIA

Standing in silence, I watch as Dante beats the shit out of Chad before turning his attention to his friends.

After peeling off his shirt and dressing the blonde, he snaps at me as he picks her up, "Venecia. We're leaving."

I follow behind him as he carries her out of VIP and over to the bar. Sitting her behind the bar, he whispers to the barkeeper while gesturing to the VIP area. Moments later bouncers are pulling the guys out of the VIP area and towards the back of the club.

"You're going to be okay," Dante bends down to the blonde, "Sarah is going to keep an eye on you until the cops get here."

Standing up, his bloodied hand wraps around mine and pulls me against his hard, sweaty body. His bare skin radiates warmth against me as he leads me from the club.

It isn't until we reach the car that he finally says anything to me, "Are you okay?"

"I'm fine," I shake my head.

His eyes narrow at my response and my body is immediately against the car. He cages me in with his arms, leaving us just inches apart.

"Fuck, Venecia," he growls at me, closing the distance between us and using his body to wedge me against the car, "You can't put yourself in those kinds of situations."

"You did your job," her voice flat as she responds, "Nothing happened."

Rough scruff brushes against my jaw before he growls in my ear, "Plenty happened. Watching him touch you, I could have fucking killed him. The thought of any man touching you, it fucking infuriates me."

His hands grab mine, pinning them over my head as he continues to bury his face in my neck, "No man is good enough to touch you, and we both know that none of them could give you what you want. What you need."

"What is it I want?" my words slow and aching as my chest heaves against his bare skin, and I press my neck into his touch. His thigh presses between my legs and rubs against my center, only furthering my need for more of his touch.

"Someone to worship you," his lips run up the side of my neck, "To please you. To put your pleasure before their own."

"Someone who will make you beg, instead of just giving you whatever you want," his lips dust over mine, "but will never leave you wanting."

"Someone," I breathe deep and swallow hard before the breathy words leave my mouth, "like you?"

"Hey," an authoritative voice yells as a flashlight shines on us, "Ma'am, everything okay?"

Dante releases my hands and steps back from me, my body suddenly cold without his warmth pressed against me.

"Ma'am?"

"Yes. Yes, officer. Everything is fine."

"Take it somewhere else then," he calls back.

Dante nods at him as he opens my door to the car, his face and demeanor instantly transformed back to the professional bodyguard with no feelings. Climbing into the backseat it is apparent that he will not be doing anything to alleviate this ache he created between my thighs.

The ride home in silence only solidifies that whatever that moment was, it is gone now.

DANTE

Everyone else went to bed hours ago. Since they left, I have been sitting in the study by myself reading and nursing a glass of whiskey.

More accurately, blindly holding a book in my hands as I think about my hands and lips all over her body as it was pressed between me and the car.

Looking down at my watch, it's nearly two in the morning. I didn't realize just how long I have been sitting here alone.

Deciding I should probably get some sleep before everyone wakes in the morning, I set my book on the coffee table. After placing my glass in the kitchen sink, I quietly make my way upstairs as to not wake anyone.

Reaching the landing, I vaguely hear a faint whimper coming from down the hall. My shoes tap on the hardwood floor as I walk down the near silent hallway. After taking a few steps, I pick up my pace when I realize that the muffled cries are coming from Venecia's room. I am about to barge through the slightly ajar door when I find the source of my concern.

The cause of my concern is more deadly than I could have imagined.

Venecia is laying on her bed. Her left knee is up, the other has fallen to the side, and the sheets have been pulled down so that they are pooling low around her thighs, granting me unfettered access to this unauthorized view of her body.

I should leave, give her the privacy she is expecting to have, but I can't turn away.

I've been dreaming about this woman coming for weeks.

I need what she is showing me, even if she isn't intending to.

Heavy breaths and quiet whimpers continue to come from her. The moonlight filtering through the window glistens over her bare skin accentuating her curves and toned muscles. Her back is arched, and her ample breasts rise and fall with each breath. Her fingers are working fervently between the slit of her shaved pussy, mercilessly rubbing her clit. Her movements quickly causing her whimpers to become quiet, breathy cries of pleasure.

As I stand in the doorway, watching the deviously forbidden things I have been dreaming about and masturbating to for weeks, my cock grows against the confines of my pants. The sudden need to stroke my cock to relieve the pressure is nearly painful. Rubbing my palm against the aching bulge in my pants, Venecia slowly turns her face towards the door. When her gaze meets the door, it feels as though Venecia's eyes meet mine. That they are staring straight into mine, urging me to watch and as her hips grind relentlessly against her hand.

From the darkness of the hallway, she can't see me. Can she?

Those blue eyes stay fixated on the gap in the door. Her thighs squeezing together as she comes hard against her own hand, her teeth biting into her bottom lip as she tries to silence her screams.

"Dante...," my name slowly whispers from her mouth as she continues to writhe against her fingers, punishing her sensitive clit while she rides out her orgasm.

My cock twitches beneath my palm as I watch her come, and I can feel the wetness of precum on my tip.

Venecia's hand reaches for the sheet, and I swear she smirks at me as she pulls it over body. In turn, I take a startled step backwards.

Did she know I was here the whole fucking time?

Turning and quickly crossing the hallway, I step into my room. Pushing the door shut behind me, I free my cock and immediately provide myself the relief I so desperately need.

It isn't until my cum splatters across my hand that I realize while I can make myself come, I can't actually provide myself the relief I am seeking.

Chapter Eleven

VENECIA

It sounds as though everyone that works for my father has been filtering into this house since before dawn, making it nearly impossible to sleep. Since this is the first time I have been awake for breakfast in weeks, I quickly shower, dress and head downstairs.

Making my way down the stairs, my opinion of all the noise wasn't exactly wrong. There are tons of guys, some I have met before and some I have never even seen, standing and chattering loudly amongst themselves, throughout the downstairs hall.

"*Abbassa i toni,*" Papa calls over everyone, "Quiet down."

All these loud, boisterous men are immediately silent and their attention promptly turned to him.

"This shit ends now," his voice bellows throughout the hall, "This family will not be seen as weak. If we don't know which family is behind this, fuck 'em all!"

I watch as Ava squeezes closer against my brother, Lorenzo. While she hasn't been with this family long, I think she is the only other person who shows any emotion at Papa's words. The concerned look on her face mirrors mine.

"Fuck 'em all," Papa repeats, "We hit them all on Monday. The Russians. The Armenians. The Triad. The Yakuza. Fucking all of them. Take the weekend, get your families situated. Monday night, we go to war."

After a few minutes of quiet, side conversations, nearly everyone has filtered out of the hallway, leaving as Papa had commanded. The only people left standing with me are Lorenzo, Ava, Papa, Luca, Carlo...and Dante.

Dante stands with this family as though he is as much a part of it as my brothers.

Papa looks at Dante approvingly, as though over the past few weeks he has proved himself worthy of being part of this family.

"Because I don't quite trust you to follow my instructions," Papa turns to me, "Dante will be watching over you until these things are situated."

"You've got to be kidding me," I huff back at him.

"I don't kid about the safety of my family. He will be taking you out of town to some place safe this afternoon."

"Seriously. I have shit planned for this week. Can't he just continue to keep an eye on me around here?"

"Venecia," Papa's voice loud and firm, "This is not up for debate. I suggest you go pack a bag."

"Fucking bullshit," I mumble under my breath before heading upstairs.

When I reach my room, I slam the door and flop onto the bed. Pulling my phone from my pocket I text Jessica.

VENECIA
> No party. All plans are off

JESSICA
> What the fuck did you do?
> WTF! Aren't you too old to get grounded.

> Right?
> Papa is sending me away for the week.
> Something about needing me out of town.

> Anywhere good?
>
> Italy?
>
> Maldives?
>
> Can I come? LOL.

Before I can respond to her again, Dante is in my room and ripping the phone from my hand. He immediately begins thumbing through my text messages.

"Hey," my hands flail at him trying to grab back my phone, "That's mine."

"Apparently you don't understand how this works," he starts typing on my phone, "if you tell everyone that you are going away and where you are going it isn't safe anymore."

"Your friend thinks you are going to London, but you leave soon and need to pack," he finishes typing, turns off my phone and shoves it into his pocket, "I will give this back to you when it's safe for you to have it."

"You don't need to treat me like a fucking child," I snap back at him.

DANTE

"You don't need to treat me like a fucking child," she snaps at me as I shove her phone into my pocket.

"You are acting like a child, and quite frankly like a fucking brat," I force the words out of my mouth, while trying to sound as though I am frustrated and annoyed with her.

"Start packing," my words still harsh as I turn to leave the room, "Sneakers, not stilettos. And we are leaving at three. You'll go with what you have if you aren't ready."

I need her to fucking hate me. To despise everything about me.

It's the only way I am going to make it.

The only way to be alone with her and not act on every depraved thought I've had for weeks.

Yet, I cannot seem to bring myself to actually do it.

Crossing the hall and entering my room, I pull one of my suitcases from the closet. After throwing Venecia's phone into my dresser, I begin packing enough clothes to be gone for a week.

As I turn towards the bathroom to grab my toiletries, I see Venecia across the hall throwing various clothes onto her bed. When she notices I am watching her, her jaw clenches, eyes narrow, and her nose wrinkles. The scowl on her face holding firm, she enthusiastically flips me off before returning to her packing.

Good. Maybe that was enough...

If I'm lucky, we'll go this whole week without her wanting to speak a word to me. She'll stay in her room. I'll make sure I keep my distance. Everything will be fine.

After spending a few more minutes gathering my things, I head downstairs. Walking into the armory, I scan the walls determining what weapons to bring with me. Once I make my decisions, I grab a duffle bag from the wall. Walking back around the room, I fill it with Keltec KS7, Mossberg 930, two Sig Sauer P30s, a Glock 17, a few KA-BAR tactical knives, and enough ammunition to take out half the city.

If shit goes sideways, I plan to be prepared.

Just as I finish putting everything into the bag, Lorenzo walks in behind me.

"So," he pauses, "what are your intentions with my sister?"

Fuck...

"My what?" I question, merely biding time to work out an answer that won't get me killed.

"What are your intentions with Venecia?" he repeats his question.

I stare back at him. The only coherent thought running through my mind is that the correct answer is not, 'bury my face in her pussy until her thighs won't stop shaking'.

Yeah, that is definitely not the right answer.

"Where do you plan on taking her?" his voice a tad gruffer as he rephrases his question.

"Oh, yeah," I flounder when I realize that was the question he was actually asking this whole time, "I was going to come and talk with you and Sal about that as soon as I was done here."

"Sal's tied up with some things, but now is a good a time as any for me."

I follow him out of the armory, hoping that my inability to answer his simple question doesn't raise any suspicions.

Dropping the duffle bag in the hall, we walk towards the study and each take a seat.

He stares at me for a moment, and I realize I should start talking.

"I know that the family has numerous safe houses in the city, but knowing what is about to happen here," I pause as Lorenzo acknowledges that destruction that is about to take over this city, "I think it's significantly safer to take her much further away."

"Good," Lorenzo nods his agreement, "I think that's a good plan."

"Considering Botticelli properties have been getting hit left and right, I also think it's best for us to be somewhere not connected to the family."

Lorenzo nods, giving his approval thus far.

"I was going to take her out of the city," I pause momentarily waiting for his refusal.

When it doesn't come, I continue, "My step father's family has an old hunting cabin not far outside of Elmira. It's secluded. It'll be easy to protect."

"Don't let anyone else know where you're going," Lorenzo stands from his seat, "Reach out if you need anything. Otherwise, we'll reach out to you when it's safe to come back. And Dante, make sure you take good care of her."

"I will."

The only thing I actually worry about keeping her safe from is me. From everything else, I will protect her with my life.

Chapter Twelve

VENECIA

Promptly at three, there is a knock at my door.

He wasn't fucking kidding.

My two bags are already packed and waiting by the door. Sitting up on the bed, I call out, "Yeah?"

The door opens and as expected, it is Dante.

"You ready?" his voice is gruff as his eyes travel down towards the bags not far from his feet.

"Yes. I just need to throw on my shoes."

"Good," his simple response as abrasive as earlier, he reaches for my heavy bags, lifting them with ease.

"I'll meet you outside at the car. I just want to say goodbye to my family first."

Nodding his head, he leaves my room, and I can hear his feet quickly tread down the hallway.

Not wanting to piss him off any further, I pull on my sandals and quickly head downstairs to see Papa and my brothers. They are so engrossed in their planning that I only get a few moments to speak with each of them.

Walking out the front door, I see Dante is waiting at the bottom of the steps, standing next to a blacked-out Tahoe. When he sees me, he opens the rear door for me to get in.

He's barked at me enough times to put on my seatbelt that I reach for it instinctually as he begins to close my door. Still, it is the first thing he checks when he climbs into the driver's seat.

Is it because of concern? Or because he expects me not to do it?

Dante turns over the ignition, and I watch out the rear window as my home slowly disappears behind me. I have left this house thousands of times, but this time feels drastically different than the rest.

We spend nearly two hours basically parked in gridlock. The inside of this car is practically silent, the only noises the engine occasionally revving and horns blaring from the other side of the windows. Interactions between us are limited and only occur for a few split seconds when our eyes meet in the rearview mirror.

As we finally start moving, I notice that we are approaching the George Washington Bridge. When we begin to cross it, I realize that we must be leaving the city.

"Where are we going?" the words soft and hesitant to leave my lips and break this silence.

"Upstate."

As the Tahoe begins to move at a progressively faster speed, Dante and I are immediately seated in uncomfortable silence again. Back to essentially pretending the other doesn't exist in this vehicle.

Staring out the window as the sun slowly approaches the tops of the trees, there is nothing but wilderness and windy roads. We left the highway soon after getting out of the city and have been driving on nearly unoccupied country roads for the past two hours. It has been at least half that long since I saw another car on the road.

After hours of it, the silence in this car is almost deafening. Turning my gaze from the window, they lock onto Dante's in the rearview mirror. Only this time, neither of us look away. While only a few seconds, it feels like an eternity before his eyes divert back to the road.

I cannot take this tension or this silence any longer. While it may have only been a few hours in this car, it has been going on for weeks.

"Are we going to pretend it didn't happen?" I push out the hesitant words, trying unsuccessfully not to let my voice crack.

"Pretend what didn't happen?" his question nearly devoid of any emotion.

"Last night," the words barely leave my mouth before his eyes are wide and completely locked on mine in the mirror again, "When you watched me from the hallway."

Dante is silent and my heart is thumping in my chest, but his eyes don't leave the reflection of mine. Swallowing my nerves, I press the button to unfasten my seatbelt before slowly dragging it back across my body.

"Venecia," his normally firm and commanding voice is unsteady, leaving us both unsure if that was his attempt at telling me to stop.

"Did you like it?" my hands push the thin straps of my dress off each of my shoulders and down my arms until the top of my dress is pooled around my waist. My breasts fully exposed to him, I pause for a moment to delicately toy with each of my nipples, both already taut from a mixture of my nerves and excitement.

"Ven-," his words cut short as he watches my fingers slowly inch the skirt of my dress over my knees until both of my thighs are fully exposed. Lifting it further, I shift my body so that I am facing him and part my thighs, revealing the sheer black lace panties barely covering me.

"Did you like it," I repeat before slowly licking my fingers to wet them with my saliva, "watching me play with my pussy until I came?"

I gasp, as the Tahoe nearly swerves off the road when I press my fingers beneath the lace and against my clit.

"I heard you in the hallway," my words quickly become increasingly breathy, in part to both my nervous excitement and the finger working between my thighs, "how heavy your breaths were as you watched me."

"Venecia," his voice both distraught and excited as I continue to tease both him and my clit.

"Because I loved knowing you were in the hallway watching."

"We can't."

"Were you wondering if I was thinking about you as you got hard for me?"

"We shouldn't," his voice wavers.

"Because I was," the words pass over my lips in a breathy moan.

His eyes are more focused on me than the road as I continue to work myself towards an orgasm.

DANTE

I struggle to keep my eyes on the road as I watch her body react to the hand rubbing beneath those thin lace panties. Her hips rock to meet her fingers, as she slowly begins to approach her orgasm.

The orgasm we both know I so desperately want to give her.

The cock throbbing in my pants a clear indicator that I want this as much as she does.

If not more...

"Fuck it," I grumble while veering to the side of the road. The speed at which we hit the gravel on the shoulder causes the SUV to fishtail slightly before we come to a stop. My seatbelt is off, and I'm opening the door as I throw the shifter into park.

The soft moans coming from her mouth are increasing, and I cannot get to her fast enough.

Slamming my door, I quickly walk behind the SUV while pulling my shirt over my head. Tossing it to the ground as I reach her door, I grab the handle and yank the door open. An aching moan comes from her mouth as I yank her hand from her panties, ending any possibility of the orgasm she was so close to before sucking her fingers into my mouth.

Finally tasting her sweet cunt on my tongue, I fucking need to have more of her. Gripping her panties with both hands, I pull hard at them. The thin lace shreds from her body, and the tattered remains are thrown to the ground with my shirt.

Lifting her slightly, I lay her across the seat while climbing in on top of her. Her tight nipples now gently dust against my chest with every heavy breath she takes.

"Is this what you want?" I pause, my face so close to hers I can feel her fluttered breathes, "*Cuore mio*. I can't take it."

"Yes," she gently exhales, "Please."

Sliding my hand under her head, I firmly grip her hair and pull her face up to meet mine. Her lips part as she reaches me, and without hesitation I plunge my tongue into her mouth. Having waited for and dreamt about this moment for weeks, I cannot get enough of tasting her. Breathing in her sighs and whimpers is like taking my first breath of real air. Both of us are panting and still yearning for more when I finally pull back from her.

A breathy moan rises from her chest when I glide my fingers over her already swollen lips. Taking advantage of her open mouth, I plunge two fingers over her lips and deep inside. Deep enough that she lets out a gentle gag before wrapping her lips around them.

"That's a good fucking girl," I groan as my lips trail down her neck while she begins to gently suck on the fingers resting on her tongue.

My tongue aggressively swirls around her nipple before I suck it into my mouth. In turn, Venecia sucks eagerly and moans against the fingers now slowly working in and out of her mouth. Her hips rocking against the hard cock in my pants trying to grant herself some relief.

"You suck like a greedy slut that can't wait to take my cock in her mouth," I slowly pull my dripping fingers from her mouth before replacing them with my tongue. My mouth continuing to needily claim each of her moans.

Tilting my hips to the side, my wet fingers slide through her soaked pussy with ease.

"Is it the thought of sucking my cock or fucking it that makes you this wet?" my fingers assault her clit leaving her unable to answer.

Drawing her nipple back into my mouth, my fingers continue to work over and around her clit. Her breaths become shallow, and her body tenses.

"Don't fight it," my finger plunges inside of her and curls, eliciting a gasp as she clenches and comes undone around it. Continuing to slowly work my curling finger in and out of her through her orgasm, I slowly slide it back to her clit as she comes down.

"Whether it's thinking about sucking my cock or fucking it that gets you this wet, you're going to have to wait," my fingers work her already sensitive clit causing raspy moans to rattle from her chest, "You have to earn it."

An airy, "what," mixed with a moan passes over her lips.

"You have to earn my cock," my fingers rub firm circles over her clit causing her back to arch, pressing her cunt against my hand as she comes again.

"I won't just give you what you want. You're going to come on my fingers or tongue until you're begging me to finally fuck you with my cock. Even then, I'm not going to give you my cock until you earn it."

Chapter Thirteen

VENECIA

"Yes," I scream as another orgasm blissfully tears through my body.

"Please," I cry out in both pleasure and pain-tinged exhaustion. I have lost track of how many times Dante has made me come with his fingers, either on my clit or buried deep inside of me. Every muscle in my body is beginning to feel fatigued from the orgasms spasming through my body.

"There we go," he says smugly while slowly unfastening his pants, "that sounds like a good girl who is ready and begging for my cock. Show me how well you beg."

"Please...I need..."

"Tell me what you need."

"I need you to fuck me with your cock."

Pulling his pants over his hips, he frees his massive erection. His finger was so tight at first; I have no idea how he is going to get that inside of me.

I am so exhausted I can barely breathe, let alone speak as I feel him pulling my leg around his hip so he can settle himself between my thighs. His tip slides over my clit eliciting a moan, before sliding down my slit and resting against my opening, where he pauses.

"Wait," my voice struggles to push out the word through my exhaustion.

With the tip of his cock resting against me, he waits a moment for me to catch my breath.

"Can you go slow at first," the words quiet and sheepish as they leave my mouth.

"Don't worry," his hand grips my hip, "you can take all of my cock."

"No," the word blurts from my mouth, before the rest of my words immediately vomit out, "That's not it. This is my first time."

"Your what?" Dante questions while quickly pushing himself off me. He struggles to tuck himself back into his pants, as though he can't get away from me fast enough. It is like he is utterly repulsed by the words that just spewed from my mouth.

"Fuck," he grumbles as he picks his shirt up off the ground.

"You need to get dressed," are the last words he says before closing the door and walking behind the car.

Slowly sitting up, every muscle in my body is screaming. Yet, the tears I am fighting back have nothing to do with how sore my body is. Grabbing the straps to my dress, I watch Dante pace along the side of the car, as my trembling hands slide them over my shoulders. Pulling the dress back over my thighs, it suddenly feels like there isn't enough fabric to cover me.

After putting on my seatbelt, my arms are wrapping around my body, in an attempt, to cover myself when Dante climbs into the front. Closing the door, he turns the ignition and sits with his hands on the wheel staring straight out the window for a moment before turning to face me.

"I'm sorry," his words flat and nearly devoid of any emotion as his eyes bore through me, "We can't do this."

Shifting his body so that he is facing forward again, he shifts into drive and pulls the SUV back onto the road. We are in complete silence again. The only difference, with the sun having set, it is dark in here and we can no longer see each other in the rearview mirror. I am grateful, because that also means that he cannot see the silent tears currently rolling down my cheeks.

After forty more unbearable minutes of silence, we pull from the asphalt onto a bumpy gravel drive. A few minutes later, we pull through a clearing and I can see the moon reflecting over the lake in front of us. Dante pulls up to a small cabin and parks.

Not wanting him to see my red eyes or splotchy face and know I was crying; I open my door and climb out of the Tahoe. Walking towards the lake, the breeze coming from the water is cool. The thin summer dress not offering much cover and a chill rattles down my spine.

"Are you okay?" the proximity of his deep voice chills me more than the breeze blowing over the lake.

Closing my eyes, I take a deep breath before turning around, because I know he is right behind me.

DANTE

Venecia slowly turns around, and I immediately see what I was expecting. Her eyes are bloodshot, her cheeks red and stained with subtle streaks of the mascara that had previously run down her face. Her face full of the unmistakable evidence of the tears she tried to silently cry in the backseat.

The tears she cried because of me.

I panicked. Panic gets a man like me killed. Yet there I was, suddenly scared shitless of what was about to happen with the woman standing in front of me.

Realizing that I am acutely aware of the physical remains of the emotions she was desperately trying to hide, Venecia attempts to turn away from me. Reaching out, I grab her arm. My grip tight enough to force her to stay and look at me.

*To allow **me** to look at her.*

When our eyes meet, I watch as her face crumbles when she is no longer able to fake her brave facade. Her vulnerability and the pain I have caused her are absolutely crushing.

Tears slowly rolling down her face, she sobs, "Did I do something wrong?"

Palming her cheeks, and using my thumbs to gently wipe away the tears, I shake my head at her, "No. You didn't do anything wrong."

"Then why?" she struggles to maintain eye contact with me. "Every guy I've ever been around has wanted to be the one to claim it."

"Those are boys, Venecia."

Smug, arrogant boys that don't know the difference between fucking their hand and pleasing a woman.

"Why didn't you tell me?"

"Why?" her voice turning angry as she steps away from me, "When I did, you couldn't get away from me fast enough.

"I'm sorry. We shouldn't have," I hesitate to continue, "I never would have pulled the car over, had I known."

"My inexperience is that fucking repulsive to you?"

Not in the least.

Before I get the opportunity to respond, she is storming towards the cabin and heading inside. The slamming door my cue that this conversation is over.

For now.

After a few deep breaths to collect my thoughts, I trek back to the Tahoe. Removing the suitcases from the back, I bring all our belongings inside. Dropping our things in the living room, I head into the kitchen. I am pleased to find that the property's caretaker received my message this morning and stocked the cabinets with a few days of food for us.

Or as he was under the impression, my brother-in-law and some fishing buddies.

Placing Venecia's bags outside of the bedroom, I grab a few things from mine before heading into the bathroom. After being so close to fucking her, I need to fucking come. Or I at least need to take a cold fucking shower.

Kicking off my shoes and removing my clothes, I realize that I smell like her. My hands have the faint aroma of her vanilla scented shampoo and her cunt.

A tight cunt I was so close to fucking.

Turning on the water, I crank the handle until steam begins fogging over the glass door. My cock is hard and already aching for the release I was denied when I decided to cock-block myself.

I just need to get it out of my system.

Stepping into the shower, I lick my fingers. I need to taste her again, to savor her sweet taste, before the water begins washing her from my skin.

Fucking delectable. So delectable that I regret not burying my face between her thighs and devouring her.

Precum drips from my tip at the thought, and I wipe it into my palm, using it as lubricant to begin fucking my fist.

The eagerness with which her mouth sucked on my fingers.

How her tight little cunt clenched around my finger as she came. Over and over as she continued to come for me.

I've fisted my cock for so long that the water has run cold. I am no closer to coming than I was when I stepped into this shower.

I don't want to be fucking my hand.

My cock still rock hard and ready to fuck, I opt to turn off the water, I dry off before throwing on sweatpants and heading to the couch. After laying a shotgun on the coffee table and tucking a Glock between the couch cushions, I lay down to get a few hours of sleep.

Chapter Fourteen

VENECIA

The sun hasn't come up yet. While I am rarely ever awake this early, I have been and lying in this bed for the past hour staring at the ceiling. I'm hesitant to get up and head out into the rest of the cabin.

Every time I think this is going somewhere, I embarrass the living hell out myself.

How the fuck am I going to face him after last night?

Fuck it. I'm tired of this pendulum with him.

It's going to have to happen sooner or later.

Throwing back the covers, I swing my legs over the edge and touch my toes to the floor. The hardwood floors are cold against my bare feet, causing me to pause for a moment before standing.

Walking towards the bedroom door, it is quiet. I don't hear Dante making any noise in the cabin. Slowly turning the knob, I gingerly pull open the door ensuring to stay quiet.

Dante is asleep on the couch, his long muscular body filling it from end to end. His bare feet are resting across the arm of the couch closest to me. His thick legs are covered by a baggy pair of sweatpants. Even in his sleep they are slung low over his hips, exposing a faint trail of hair between the deep V-lines drawing my eyes back down towards the bulge in his pants.

Tiptoeing closer to him, my eyes are glued to his rippled abs and firm chest. As if it isn't impressive enough, it's flanked with perfectly sculpted arms and shoulders.

The normally combed-back black hair is currently falling over his face as he sleeps. Unlike when he is awake, his face looks soft and gentle. In this moment, the only thing currently rough about it is the few days of scruff growing along his jaw.

Reaching my hand out, my fingers slowly inch towards him to gently brush some of the hair out of his face. The moment I touch him, he firmly wraps one hand around my wrist and the other around my throat. As much as I want to scream, the fingers gripping my throat would make it impossible.

His grip tightens painfully as he quickly rises from the couch and throws my body onto the coffee table, his landing on top of mine. Looking down at me, his eyes are wide as he immediately releases the grip on my throat, his fingers lingering softly around my neck.

His body still firmly on top of me, he uses his free hand to gently brush the hair from my face before softly asking, "Are you okay? I didn't realize it was you."

I nod and my eyes blink at him, but with his hand around my throat and body laying firmly on top of mine I am unable to make a coherent thought.

Dante shifts his weight slightly and I suddenly feel his erection pressing firmly against me before he lifts himself off me.

"I thought me and my virginity were repulsive," the words smug as my eyes travel towards the erection barely being contained by his baggy sweatpants.

"I never once said you repulsed me," he reaches his hand out to assist me off the table.

Hesitantly, I take it as he continues, "I said we can't do this. I didn't say I didn't want to."

"I don't understand," I unsuccessfully try to pull my hand from his as he sits on the couch pulling me down next to him.

"The way you act. The comfort you have with your body. The way you so brazenly stripped down and tempted me last night. I had assumed that you were more...well...experienced."

"Papa and my brothers-," he interrupts my words, a sad attempt to explain, by gently grabbing my jaw.

"I never would have pulled over had I known," his hand tucks my hair behind my ear when I fidget uncomfortably at his words.

"Just let me finish," his fingers linger down the side of my neck and I silently nod at him to continue.

"I am almost old enough to be your father. I am not like the childish boys you're used to," his fingers continue to travel over my shoulder and gently down my bare arm, "Believe me when I tell you that I wanted to fuck you last night. The urge to fuck you, to feel you, to own your body consumes my fucking mind."

"Then," I hold back the words while I wait for my bottom lip to stop trembling.

"Then why didn't I?" Dante poses my own question, "Because I wanted to, but you deserve better. So much better. Not getting fucked in the backseat on the side of the road by someone making you beg for it."

"What is it you think I deserve?"

Pulling his hand back from my arm, he stands up, "Something I can't give you. Someone soft. Someone who is going to be gentle with you."

Something in his words sets a fire in me.

Maybe it's a lifetime of the constant men in my life treating me as though they need to be soft and gentle with me.

Standing up my hands slap against his bare chest as I shove him, his body taking a step back more out of shock than the impact of my push.

"Contrary to popular belief, I'm not a delicate glass princess that needs to be handled with care," I step close and place my hands on his chest to shove him again, "You are the first person in my life who didn't treat me like you were afraid I was going to break."

"I shouldn't ha-," his words cut short as I shove him again and his back presses against the wall.

I watch as his brows furrow and his eyes narrow.

"You weren't afraid I was going to break," I step to him again, this time to close the distance between us.

"Had I known, I never would have-"

"I have enough people being gentle with me," I press my body against his until there is no longer any space between us, "I want you to try to fucking break me."

DANTE

Venecia's body is pressed against mine. She steps closer and I can feel her tight nipples pressing against my chest through the thin material of her shirt. Looking up at me, I am so fixated on her mouth that I barely hear the words she speaks, "I want you to try to fucking break me."

"You don't know what you're asking," I stare back down at her.

Her blue eyes just stare back up at me, while her pouty bottom lip protrudes slightly, undoubtedly at the thought of me rejecting her again.

"I **will** break you," her body tenses and her eyes widen slightly at my words. My hands fist and claw at the sides of my thighs, as I struggle not to put them on her.

Venecia's body stays firm against mine and those unwavering eyes continue to stare up at me. Every ounce of her small stature urging and daring me to make good with my promise. It is as though she is not even the slightest bit hesitant.

As much as they should, it isn't her family that makes me hold back. It's me.

"Look me in the eyes and tell me you don't feel something between us," she continues to stare up at me, her eyes completely locked with mine.

I want to deny her, do the right thing, and tell her that I feel absolutely nothing towards her. But my mouth cannot form the words.

"Look me in the eyes and tell me you don't want this, Dan-."

Before she has a chance to finish, my hands are fisting the hair at the nape of neck and pulling her mouth towards mine. My tongue aggressively pushing between her lips and assaulting her mouth. Her tongue intertwines with mine as I continue vigorously exploring her mouth.

She releases an airy whimper into my mouth, causing my still hard cock to throb against her.

"I can't deny that I want you," the words grumble from my mouth as I pull on her hair granting me better access to her neck. My lips and tongue make my way down her long neck as she groans, a mixture of pleasure and pain.

"I will push you," my lips trail upwards feeling her rapid pulse beneath the thin skin of her neck, "I get off on it. I will push your body and your mind until you are ready to break."

Gently biting on her neck, the pounding beat of her heart can be felt vibrating on my tongue.

Releasing my mouth from her neck, I raise my head until we make eye contact again. The look in her eyes is hungry as she stares back into mine.

"And you will be mine," the words firm and demanding as they leave my mouth.

"If that is what you actually want," my hands gently tug on the fistfuls of her hair causing her mouth to gape open, "I'm going to need to hear you say it."

"Please," she begs softly, "I want this."

Releasing her hair, my hands travel down her back and over the curve of her ass until they make their way to her thighs. Gripping them both, I lift until her legs are wrapping around my waist.

Turning us both, I press her against the wall. Using my hips as leverage to help hold her in place, my hands grip the hemline of her shirt, pulling it over her head, and exposing her perky breasts. Gripping one firmly with my right hand, I roll her taut nipple between my thumb and forefinger. In response, her back arches causing her hips to grind against mine.

"Oh, *cuore mio*," I grind back into her continuing to toy with her nipple until a gentle, whimper trembles from her lips.

"I'll go easy on you this time," I pause to pull her nipple into my mouth, flicking it with my tongue and sucking until I elicit a moan, "but you're still going to be begging for my cock before I fuck you."

Firmly gripping her ass and pulling her from the wall, I carry her across the room before delicately laying her on the couch. Climbing between her thighs, my face is immediately buried between her tits.

"Before last night, have you ever had a man kiss you here," my fingers and mouth continue alternating between teasing each of her nipples while I grind my throbbing cock against the apex of her thighs.

She is silent.

Shifting my eyes from her heaving breasts to her face, I see her cheeks are pinking and she is embarrassingly shaking her head.

Chapter Fifteen

VENECIA

"Before last night, have you ever had a man kiss you here?" Dante's lips, tongue, teeth, and fingers continue to play with my nipples as I sheepishly shake my head at him.

"Good," he continues teasing me. Each flick, nibble and pinch shooting through my nerves and straight to my clit. My body is trembling as my hips grind against the massive erection he has pressed between my thighs.

"Not yet," his voice deep and gravelly as his lips slowly trail down my stomach, his stubble scratching against my sensitive skin. His eyes locked onto mine; his tongue slowly dips into my navel as his fingers slip under the elastic band of my shorts.

His lips continue to kiss across my stomach as he makes his way to the sensitive skin at the crease of my hips. As his lips travel my untouched skin, his fingers slowly begin dragging my shorts and panties down my legs. Once he passes them over my feet, I am laying naked beneath him.

"Has a man ever kissed you here," his finger slides through my slit collecting my arousal.

His eyes are still fixed on me as I shake my head.

"That means your sweet, little, wet cunt is mine, and it will only ever be mine," his voice sounds pleased.

Dante slowly pushes himself off me until he is sitting on his feet between my thighs. Reaching over me, he gently grabs my hands and pulls them down my body towards my hips.

"Open up for me," his hands wrap behind my thighs, forcefully pushing them towards my hips, "Hold them open. I want to admire this beautiful, shaved, pink pussy."

With my hands behind my knees, I hold my thighs open while Dante's eyes roam over every inch of me. My body is trembling, a mixture of my current state of vulnerability and nervous excitement for the eternity it takes for him to touch me again. When he does, his fingers slide over my entrance, through my slit and over my clit before putting it to his lips.

Pushing it into his mouth, he sucks so hard his cheeks draw in. A growl grumbles in his chest, as he sucks my wetness from his finger.

"If you come for me like a good girl," his finger slides inside of me while his thumb rubs over my clit, "I'll kiss this sweet cunt and suck your clit until you are begging me to stop."

His finger firmly curls inside of me, as his thumb continues to caress over my clit. Both working in rhythm, my body is tight and ready to explode.

"If you want my tongue lapping at your clit," his lips dust over my thigh as the rhythm of his movements becomes faster and harder, "you're going to need to show me just how badly you actually want it."

A breathy scream rattles from my lungs as the orgasm begins to shoot through me.

Still trembling through my release, the faint whisper of, "that's a good girl," is the last thing I hear before his tongue is on licking vigorously at my clit.

"Fuck...," I exhale, as the foreign feeling of the soft, warmness of his tongue runs over clit.

Even with the finger inside of me slowing drastically, the sensation is too much. My hips are riding against his tongue, trying desperately to relieve myself, grinding hard against him trying to come again.

I come against his face, hard. It doesn't slow him. Instead, he increases the suction with his mouth and begins firmly curling his finger against my walls. I never truly come down from the orgasm, it just continues to course through me. To continue to build in strength. The need for it to crest is almost painful.

My thighs are shaking so hard that I can no longer hold them, and they slip from my hands. The growl that erupts from Dante, as they firmly wrap around his head, throws me over the edge and my whole body spasms as the orgasm fires through every nerve in my body. My whole body is still shaking as he unwraps my legs from his head, revealing a proud smirk on his arousal coated face.

"I do love the feeling of your thighs clamped around my face," his hand wipes some of my arousal from scruff on his chin as he stands from the couch.

He sheds his sweats and boxers. The erection he releases from them looks even larger than it did last night. If was I was currently able to catch my breath, the sight of it would likely have taken my breath away.

"I know you're tired," his body presses against mine as he repositions himself between my legs, "but I am going to need one more out of you. Can you give me one more, *cuore mio*?"

The answer has barely left my lips before his tip is pressed against my entrance.

"Relax," his lips gently dust over mine. Gently taking my mouth with his tongue, still coated with the taste of me, the head of his cock presses into me before he stills. I wince as my body stretches painfully to accommodate his width.

Pulling back from the kiss, his fingers brush the sweaty hair from my face. His eyes are fixed on mine as he slides himself inside of me, moving slowly until his hips are pressed firmly against me.

"I'm going to be gentle," he slowly pulls from me, "but when I am done you will know that your cunt belongs to me. Only to me."

DANTE

Even with how wet she is, it is a struggle to press my tip into her tight little cunt. Once it is in, I fight the urge to immediately shove the length of me inside of her, giving her the time she needs to adjust to me. Needing more of her, I gently press the rest of me into her until my cock is buried inside of her.

"I'm going to be gentle," I give her a soft kiss before beginning to slowly pull out of her. From the look on her face, even stretching her with my fingers first, taking me is going to hurt a little, "but when I am done you will know that your cunt belongs to me."

She is so fucking tight that beginning to thrust in and out of her, even at a slow tempo, is indescribably perfect. Every push and pull feels like she is trying to milk the cum from my cock.

"You're so fucking wet. And tight," I moan into her ear, "and you feel so fucking good wrapped around my cock."

Too fucking good.

I'm pretty sure she is going to do me in well before I am ready to come. Burying myself deep inside of her, I nearly still my thrusts while gently kissing at the side of her neck. In turn her body arches, pressing her neck firmly into my lips.

A growl grumbles from my chest against the skin above her collarbone, the urge to relentlessly pound my cock into her nearly unbearable.

"Let me know if it's too much."

"I'm okay," she mumbles back against my lips as my hips slowly rock against her body.

Venecia's body gradually relaxes a little and I begin to set a slow, consistent pace. The look of slight discomfort on her face slowly changes to one of pleasure as my cock begins to steadily rub over her already sensitive g-spot.

"Can you handle more?" I whisper into her ear as her hips begin rocking to meet mine.

"Yes," she whimpers back through her labored breaths.

"Tell me you want more. Beg for it," my lips trail along her neck as my right hand grips her ass, "Beg to come. Beg, and I'll give you more."

"Please, Dante," her voice soft and pleading as she arches against me, "Please...I want to come. I want to give you one more."

"*Cuore mio*," my words a mere groan against her neck. In response, my thrusts slowly become deeper and harder, just like each of her breaths as she approaches her orgasm. Her thighs squeeze against my sides and she clenches painfully tight around my cock as she screams out her release.

So close behind her, I quickly pull out and wrap my hand around my cock. Staring down at her, my hand quickly slides my length coated in her arousal. It only takes a few seconds until cum shoots in thin, pale ribbons across her tanned stomach and I grunt through my release, "Fuck."

As I climb from the couch, her satiated and exhausted body barely moves. Bending down to grab my sweatpants off the floor, I place a soft kiss on her forehead before using them to clean my cum off of her. Quickly wiping off myself, I toss them back to the floor, "That'll do for now."

"Can you walk? Or do you want me to carry you?"

With groggy eyes, she lifts her head from the couch. Taking her sluggishness as a response, my arms slide under her body before pulling her up to my chest. Her exhausted body melts into mine as I carry her to the bedroom.

Continuing to hold her tight against my chest, I lay us both onto the bed. Brushing her hair from her face, my lips press against her forehead, "*Cuore mio*," her eyes fall shut as we lay in a pile of tangled limbs.

Chapter Sixteen

VENECIA

Groggily, I feel around the bed as I wake up to realize that I am alone. Pulling the blanket from the bed, I wrap it around my naked body as I go to find Dante.

The smell of freshly made pancakes and bacon overwhelms me when I open the bedroom door.

"Dante?"

"In here," he calls out as he steps into the kitchen doorway. He is shirtless, the sun peeking through the windows detailing every bulge and ripple of his chiseled body. A pair of baggy grey sweatpants are sitting low on his hips again, accentuating his insanely cut Adonis belt. My eyes follow the v-line to the bulge in his pants. I gently chew my bottom lip to distract me from the soreness aching between my thighs.

"Hungry?" he cheekily lifts a brow and gestures for me to sit at the table.

"I'm good."

"You need to eat," he scoops scrambled eggs next to the bacon and pancakes already on the plates before placing them on the table and taking a seat.

"I'm not hungry," I politely decline, while walking towards the freshly brewed coffee on the counter.

"Come here," his voice suddenly deeper and more demanding.

Abruptly turning around, I am met with his furrowed brow and a slight scowl.

"I wasn't asking," his hand taps on his thigh.

"So, you're just going to tell me what to do now?"

"Sometimes," he stands from the table, steps towards me and places his hands on my face, "I think I was very clear earlier. You are mine now."

My mouth gapes a little.

"I will ensure you are taking care of yourself."

I am literally at a loss for words.

"Come. Sit," he pulls me to the table and onto his lap before pouring syrup over both of our plates.

Cutting a piece from my pancake, he brings it to my lips. When they part, he delicately slips it onto my tongue.

"Good girl," his lips trail against my ear causing my thighs to clench, "You need to eat. Your body is going to need the strength for the things I have planned for you."

The pancake catches in my throat at his words, and I let out a cough.

His left hand slides under the blanket and trails up my thigh while he continues to eat. His fingers graze over the crease of my hip before he places his hand on my stomach, gently holding me to him while we eat.

"I was gentle with you earlier and I took it easy on you," he pulls the blanket from around me as his hand slides over my navel and between my thighs, "I won't be this time. Consider it your punishment for refusing breakfast."

His fingers pinch my clit, causing me to yelp and squirm on his lap.

If I was wearing panties, I am pretty sure they would be soaked right now.

Dante nonchalantly carries on eating his breakfast, while his fingers between my thighs continue to gently play with my clit.

"Along with begging and earning the right to come with me," his finger dips inside of me before returning my arousal to my clit and demanding, "you will listen to me. Now eat."

"Okay," I fumble out the word while trying to push his hand from between my legs, "I'm eating."

"No, *cuore mio*," the words deep and firm as his finger slowly continues to make teasing circles around my clit.

"I can't eat," my words skirmish through his movements, "with you doing that."

"You can," his voice gravelly next to my ear, "and you'll finish it if you want to come."

Picking up my fork, I somehow struggle through eating the eggs on my plate. Picking at the pancake on my plate, my hips involuntarily begin to press against his hand, trying to help bring myself to an orgasm.

Placing his fork on his plate, he wraps his free arm around my waist and firmly pulls me against him. His grip is tight over my hips, holding me still.

"You haven't earned it yet," the fingers on my clit become teasingly light, "you still need to finish."

DANTE

"You still need to finish," the pad of my finger barely dusts over her clit. Her hips pull against my arm trying desperately to reach my touch as I continue to tease her.

It took her nearly ten minutes to eat the scrambled eggs on her plate. In that time her arousal has dampened the thigh of my sweatpants, and I have edged her twice.

"The longer it takes you to eat," I plunge two fingers inside of her, "the longer I am going play with you. The longer I'm going to bring you the edge and deny you what you so desperately want."

Grabbing the syrup from the table, I dribble a few drops between her neck and shoulder. My mouth waters as I watch the sticky beads trail down her chest. My fingers pinch her nipple to catch a drop as it is about to roll from her, and her head tips back while a moan rattles from her chest.

"You're going to be a sticky, dripping mess by the time I let you come."

"Please," she begs as I suck the drop of syrup from my finger.

"You say 'please' like such a good girl," I drip more syrup on her shoulder, "but you haven't earned it yet. You need to eat."

She pokes at the remaining food on her plate and the syrup begins to slowly trickle down her back. Gently pushing her forward, I bend to catch it with my tongue. Firmly pressing it to her skin, her thighs squeeze against my leg as I slowly lick the stickiness from her skin, my fingers playing with her clit again.

"Just a few more bites," my fingers linger down her arm until I reach her hand, helping her put more food on her fork before picking up the syrup again, "Are you going to finish? How badly do you want to finish?"

She puts the full fork into her mouth as I place the bottle of syrup against her jaw. Squeezing it gently, I draw a sticky line down her neck until I reach the edge of her shoulder. I make a similar line on the other side of her neck as she reaches for another bite of food. The syrup begins to drip down her chest and back, covering her in a shroud of stickiness, as she puts the last bite of food in her mouth.

Patiently, I wait for her to chew and swallow the last bite of food. I look back at her with pride when her needy eyes meet mine. Her eyes are pleading with me. She doesn't need to speak for me to know what she wants, but she's going to.

"You're going to need to tell me what you want," my fingers flick over her clit.

"Dante...please," her words so needy it is as though am denying her the air she needs to breathe, "Please let me come. Please."

My fingers firmly rub over her clit, her hips writhing on my leg as she chases her much needed release. She is so needy from my denial that it barely takes a minute for her to come. Screams leave her and for a moment the tenseness in her body softens.

A moment quickly taken from her as I continue my assault on her clit.

I want more of her screams. I need them.

When I finally stop, she is a trembling, sweaty mess on my lap and has soaked the leg of my pants.

Lifting her with me as I stand, my free hand pushes the dishes, which are in front her, before bending her exhausted body over the table. Holding her with one hand, I quickly pull my sweats down enough to free my hard cock.

Placing it against her entrance, I still for a second before shoving the length of me into her soaking wet cunt. She moans against the table as I quickly fill and stretch her. Bending over, I lick the syrup from her back as I slowly thrust my cock in and out of her.

"I told you," my hips bury my cock deep inside of her, "I'm not going to be gentle this time."

"You wanted to come," a whimper escapes her as I forcefully thrust into her again, "and now you're going to come until I think you've had enough."

Grabbing her hands, I stretch her arms over the length of the table stretching out her body. Licking the syrup from her back, my thrusts become deeper and more vigorous. Each plunge rattles the plates on the table and elicits a scream from Venecia.

She squeezes hard around my cock as she comes, her grip nearly causing me to come. Pulling out of her, I flip her over on the table. Her tits are glistening with the sticky syrup smeared all over her chest. Grabbing her thighs, I yank her to the edge of the table before impaling her with my cock again.

Chapter Seventeen

VENECIA

Flipping me over, Dante slams into me again. His fingers drag through the syrup on my chest before he plunges them deep into my mouth. So deep I almost gag on them. Knowing what he wants, I lick and suck the sticky sweetness from him as he begins working in and out of me.

His fingers slowly pull from my mouth. Grabbing my hand, he rubs it through the syrup pooling between my breasts before taking my fingers into his mouth. His tongue laps over them and he sucks them clean as he grabs hold of my thighs. With my legs draped over his arms, he is using them as leverage to relentlessly pound into me. My back arches from the table as another orgasm rips through my body causing me to scream out his name.

"I fucking love how you scream my name," his thumb rubs over my clit, "Do it again."

It didn't seem possible, but he picks up his pace as his thumb rubs my over-sensitive clit. Dante grunts with each relentless thrust, every muscle of my legs trembling in his arms. He continues until my legs are violently shaking and I am screaming his name through my release.

He quickly pulls himself from me and thrusts his cock on top of me. A roar releases from his chest as I watch him come across my stomach. His body collapses on mine, syrup, sweat, and his cum smearing between our bodies as he nuzzles his face into my neck until both of our breathing has slowed.

Dante places a wet, gentle kiss on my lips before standing up and pulling our sticky bodies apart. We are both a complete mess.

"Let's get you cleaned up," he pulls his sweats back over his hips, lifts me from the table and carries me to the bathroom.

"I can walk," I look up while gently pushing away from him.

"No," he sets my feet on the bathroom floor and smirks as he immediately grabs my unsteady body, "you can't."

Ensuring he continues to hold me steady, he reaches around me and turns on the shower before removing his sweats. After checking the water, he grabs a washcloth and walks me into the shower where he places us both in the warm spray of the water. Once we are both rinsed off, he begins to delicately scrub the wet, soapy washcloth over my skin. He meticulously cleans every inch of me, removing all evidence of the sticky mess made in the kitchen before he washes himself and drops the washcloth to the floor of the shower.

Dante gingerly removes the elastic holding my messy bun in place, and my hair cascades down my back. Moving my head under the spray of the water, he wets my hair before using his fingertips to lather shampoo in it. Being careful not to get water in my face, he rinses it clean and repeats the process with conditioner. Ensuring I stay in the warm spray of the water, he quickly shampoos his own hair before turning off the water.

Stepping out of the shower into the chilly bathroom, he grabs a towel and wraps me in it, before grabbing one for himself.

"Are you okay to go get dressed," he places a soft kiss on my lips, "or do you want me to help you?"

"I'm okay," my eyes pan up to his, "I can do it by myself."

Leaving the bathroom, I walk to the bedroom and shut the door the door behind me.

DANTE

Venecia has been lingering in the bedroom for quite a while. In the time that she has been in there, I have dressed and cleaned up most of the kitchen – both the dishes and our mess. Putting the syrup away, I'm pretty sure that I will never look at pancakes quite the same way again.

Or be able to eat them without getting hard.

As the door rattles shut on the refrigerator, I hear the bedroom door slowly creak open. A moment later, Venecia is standing in the doorway of the kitchen, with her eyes focused on the floor. Her eyes on the floor as I approach her. She only looks up when my hand cups her jaw.

"What's wrong, *cuore mio*?"

Her eyes meet mine and she looks as though she is about to cry.

"Talk to me," my words soft and urging, "tell me what is wrong."

"I...," her eyes break contact with mine, "I don't...we can't actually do this."

"Do what?"

"This," her hand bounces between our chests, "You know we shouldn't. We both know they won't let us. And it's going to kill me to have to forget about this."

Pulling her body against mine, my hands cup the sides of her face as I kiss her slow and deep. She is breathless and her lips are red when I pull back from her.

"It's my job to risk my life for you, *cuore mio*. I risk it for money," still holding her face as I stare deep into her blue eyes, "but I will happily give my life for the opportunity to have had your heart."

"Dante..."

"We aren't going to think about that now," my hands grip her ass and pull her up around my waist. Kissing her, I walk us towards the couch. Holding onto her, when I sit, she straddles my lap.

"You are mine," my fingers tuck a loose strand of hair behind her ear, "and when I take you home, I would rather die than not be able to touch you again."

"You and I both know that might happen," she whispers as her arms wrap around my neck as her head lays on my shoulder. My hands slide over her back and wrap equally as tight around her. We sit on the couch, holding each other, simply enjoying the comfort of each other's touch.

* * *

The entire weekend is spent getting to know each other, and it is passing way too quickly.

My fingers have touched every inch of her skin, and my mouth has had the pleasure of tasting it. I cannot get enough of her sweet cunt, both tasting it and how tightly it wraps around my cock.

While we may come from two very different worlds, it is as though we fill a void in each other and have a comfort that comes with knowing someone your whole life. Every minute not spent exploring her body, we've spent talking. Hours were spent discussing the bond we share over the losses of our parents when we were young. At this point, I feel as though there is nothing that I do not know about her – the extent to which the family protects her, how she has no idea what she wants to do with her life, and how badly she has needed someone in her life to not treat her like a fragile princess. I've shared my past with her – my life before the family, the years I spent at Rikers for the family, and the man I want to be for her.

Chapter Eighteen

VENECIA

It's a little after two in the morning when I wake up on the couch. I must've fallen asleep waiting to hear from my family to ensure everyone made it home safely after the attacks against the other families tonight.

Grabbing the throw from the back of the couch, I wrap it around my shoulders before heading outside to the front porch. Stepping out into the chilly summer night, I find Dante sitting in a rocking chair staring out to the lake. He has a glass of whiskey in one hand, an unlit cigar in the other, and his cell phone sitting on the table beside him.

"It'll be a few hours still," he turns to me when he hears the door close, "I'll wake you if anything goes wrong."

"I don't think I'm going to be able to go back to sleep. I'll stay out here with you while we wait to hear from them," I cross the creaky porch to him and lean on the railing across from him as look towards his view of the lake, "It's absolutely beautiful out here at night."

In a comfortable silence we both stare out over the lake, watching the reflection of the moon and the stars dance across the surface.

"There are several reasons why this is one of my favorite places, but it doesn't come close to comparing with your beauty, *cuore mio*."

After a few long sips of his whiskey, Dante's eyes travel over my body – a lusty look that I have quickly learned what follows.

"Are you wearing panties under that dress?" the deepness of his voice sends butterflies straight to my core.

Even though I left them off as he had requested earlier, my cheeks pinken at the question as I shake my head.

"Show me," his voice rough as he rocks backwards in his chair.

Gathering the bottom of my dress into my hands, I slowly slide it up my thighs, stopping just before I prove my answer.

"Don't tease me," his voice is gravelly as he rocks forward and puts his elbows on his thighs, "because we both know you will not like when I tease you in return."

Lifting it the rest of the way, I expose myself to him and he moans approvingly while sipping from his glass.

"Take off the dress," his eyes stare into mine, "Take it off and show me what that sweet little pussy of mine likes."

Pulling the dress over my head, the cool summer night air immediately tightens my already hardening nipples. Parting my legs, I use my hand to spread myself open for him, the cool air causing my clit to tingle. Drawing the fingers of my other hand into my mouth, I thoroughly coat them with saliva. As I pull them from my mouth, a frail thread of saliva keeps them connected to my mouth.

My lubricated fingers glide over my clit with ease, eliciting a never-ending string of whimpers. Keeping my fingers firmly focused on my clit, my legs quickly begin to tremble. As the orgasm creeps closer, my head rolls back. Dante drops his glass on the table and rubs at his enlarged cock through his pants.

Seeing just how excited watching me makes him, only makes me want to work my clit harder. When I am getting close to coming, he stands up and rasps out his command, "Slow. Slow down."

"Don't make yourself come," he crosses the porch and stands next to me, his hands roaming over my hips and thighs, as I struggle to follow his directions and slowly continue to play with my clit.

"I'm going to let you come once," Dante drops to his knees in front of me, "but you will earn the rest of them. Do you understand?"

Before I can answer, his face dives between my thighs and his tongue immediately laps at my clit. The gentle flicks quickly become a mixture of vigorous sucking and firm licks, leaving my legs trembling as I ride his face. I grab the railing behind me as my legs begin to struggle at their job of holding me up. Digging my nails into the railing and crying out as I come, I feel something unfamiliar – like a firm, cold finger – breech my entrance. It presses deep inside of me as I ride out the last of my orgasm.

Dante leans back from me, the evidence of my arousal coating his scruff glimmers in the moonlight. My eyes widen a little as I watch him slowly pull a cigar from inside of me. Grabbing the blanket from the porch, he stands and walks back to his chair. As he sits, he drops the blanket at his feet.

When he reaches for the table, I expect him to grab his drink. Instead, he picks up the cutter and clips the end of his cigar. Slowly putting it up to his lips, he lights it and takes a deep draw until the freshly cut tip has an even glow. A ravenous moan expels from his lungs with the billow of smoke.

"If you want to come again," he takes another deep draw and spreads his legs wide, "you're going to suck my cock while I suck the taste of your sweet cunt from this cigar."

DANTE

Venecia walks towards me, dropping to her knees on the blanket between my feet. Her eyes fixed on mine, her fingers slowly undo my belt buckle before she pulls the belt from my pants.

Fuck...

"Such a good fucking girl," my fingers trail down her face before reaching for my glass of whiskey and taking a slow, savory sip, "but can you suck my cock like a dirty little whore?"

Her fingers undo my button and lower my zipper slowly to toy with me. Gripping the waist of my pants and boxer briefs, she yanks on them freeing my hard cock and wrapping her hand around the base.

My mouth wraps around the cigar as her lips slide over the head of my cock. A groan vibrates from my chest as her tongue swirls around my tip. She continues to play with the tip, occasionally taking a little more of me into her mouth, while fisting my cock.

The air lingering around us smells of the sweet tobacco of my cigar and fragrant vanilla scented shampoo Venecia uses.

"That's how a good girl sucks a cock," I grab her hair and pull her mouth from me, "I said I wanted mine to be sucked by a dirty little whore. Now open wide and relax so I can show you how swallow my cock, *cuore mio*."

Putting the cigar in my mouth, I grab the base of my cock with my free hand and place my tip on her tongue. Still fisting her hair, I push until I can feel my tip on the back of her tongue. Drawing on the cigar, I push her over my length and hold her there until I feel her gag at the sensation of me in her throat. Lifting her, I feel her suck air into her lungs as I blow smoke from mine.

Pushing her head back down, my length presses into her throat again. When she begins eagerly taking me from tip to base and back, I release my grip on her hair. Continuing to draw on the cigar, I watch her repeatedly swallow me so vigorously that she gags nearly every time she takes me in.

"If you keep sucking like that," I moan, "my little whore is going to have a mouth full of cum."

My words don't deter her, and she continues to bob over my cock, "Do you want me to fill your mouth with cum?"

Sitting up between my legs, her eyes look up at me. She is fucking beautiful with mascara running down her face and spittle all over her chin.

"Do you want to cum on my tongue," she opens her mouth and slowly pokes out her tongue, "and fill my mouth? Or do I need to beg for it?"

"Cuore mio," I groan while pushing her mouth back over my length, "I want nothing more than to fill all your holes with my cum. I will happily start with your mouth."

She begins to greedily suck and swallow my length as though she cannot wait for me to coat her tongue. My fingers tightly fist her hair as my cock begins to twitch in her mouth, "Fuck," I cry out while pumping cum into her mouth.

Using her hair as leverage, I pull her from my cock, up to my mouth, and kiss her deep. My tongue explores her mouth, gathering the lingering taste of my salty release.

"Mmmm," I groan into her mouth before pulling away, "You did so good, *cuore mio*. You earned the right to come several more times tonight. Now, do you want me to reward you like the good girl you are or the dirty little whore you want to be?"

She stares back at me for a moment contemplating her answer to my question. Standing naked before me with a newfound confidence, she responds, "You always fuck me like a good girl. I want you to use me like your whore."

I cannot stop the smile from spreading across my face at her words. Turning briefly to balance the cigar on my empty glass, I stand from the rocking chair and walk towards her. Gripping her shoulders and spinning her around, I push her body towards the railing.

"Bend over and grab the railing," I drop to my knees behind her as she does exactly as she was told, "and spread your feet."

As she spreads her feet apart, I move my body between her legs until my face is merely inches from her. Firmly gripping her hips, I pull her pussy to my mouth before sliding my tongue through her slit. My tongue dances over her clit while I hold her firmly against my face. My face dripping with her arousal, I continue to lap at her until she comes again.

Her legs shaking, my tongue travels through her slit, from her clit and between the curvaceous cheeks of her ass. A strange, whimpered moan comes from her mouth as she feels the foreignness of my tongue circling around her puckered hole. Her back arches and presses back against me as though she has to have more of my tongue on her.

"I see my dirty little whore likes to have a tongue playing in her ass," I stand behind her replacing flicks of my tongue with the rubbing of my finger, "I bet she would love to have a cock in it."

"Please," she whines, so eager to play her role as my whore and be a good girl for me.

"Not tonight, *cuore mio*," I slide my thumb into her slick cunt until it is coated in her arousal, "but I'll let you see just how good it'll feel."

Pressing my lubricated thumb against her puckered hole, I slowly pushes it inside and begin to grow hard as she lets out an airy gasp. I watch her fingers tightly grip the railing and her back arch as I slowly works my thumb in and out her ass.

"Watching how eagerly you to take me in your ass makes me so fucking hard again for you," my voice a deep whisper before I shove the full length of my hard cock into her. Venecia lets out a raspy groan when I quickly bottom out inside of her.

My thumb and cock work the two holes in tandem, leaving Venecia a writhing and screaming mess beneath me.

"I cannot wait to shove my cock in this tight little hole," I groan as she comes clenching her walls hard around my cock, "and to pump it full of my cum."

"Yes, Dante," she screams out, shoving back into my thrusts as I continue to slam into both of her holes.

"Fuck, *cuore mi-*," I groan as my hips sputter against her while I unload inside of her. Slowly pulling my thumb from her ass, my body collapses onto her back. My lips gently pepper wet kisses on her spine while I slowly go soft inside of her, "I shouldn't have done that...I shouldn't have come in you."

"We shouldn't have done a lot of things," she mumbles back as my cock inevitably retreats from her, my cum and her arousal slowly beginning to drip down her thighs.

Her exhausted body is slumped on the porch railing. Scooping her up into my arms, I grab the phone from the table before carrying her inside to the bathroom and sitting on her on the counter.

After washing my hands, I grab a washcloth and clean her makeup-stained face before cleaning the cum from her legs.

"They will call if anything goes wrong," I take her hand and pull her towards the bedroom, "You need to get some sleep."

Chapter Nineteen

DANTE

The phone buzzing across the nightstand wakes me from my sleep. The sun blazing through the windows is nearly blinding, making it obvious that I had slept a lot longer than I had intended. The phone buzzes again. Picking it up, there four missed calls from Sal and several unread text messages.

SAL

Pick up!

Take care of her!

She's my baby

MARCO

Those assholes hit the house

SAL

LUCA
> Protect her at all costs

> They took Avalie

> Renzo is losing his fucking mind

LORENZO
> Don't let anything happen to V

CARLO
> Keep my sister safe

MARCO
> Shit is about to get crazy around here

SAL
> I'll let you know when it's safe to come home

"Fuck," I mumble while scrambling from the bed to pull on my pants.

"What is it," Venecia groggily asks with her face still buried in her pillow.

The warped floorboard by the kitchen creeks, immediately drawing my attention, and my hand instinctively grabs for the Glock sitting on the nightstand.

"What's wrong?" her eyes quickly realizing my sudden concern.

"Shhhh," my finger rises to my lips as I motion for her to get out of the bed.

She grabs the sheet and quickly wraps it around her body.

Another creak of the floorboard.

That's two.

"Get in the closet," I whisper.

She whispers back, "You're scaring me," and the fear is more than apparent in her eyes.

"Good. Take this," I shove the pistol into her hands, "If anyone but me opens this door, you pull that trigger and don't stop. Understand?"

Her eyes are teary as she nods back at me, "Dante?"

"I told you," I quickly kiss her lips before closing the closet door, "I will give my life to protect you, *cuore mio.*"

Quickly crossing the room, I grab a knife and the other pistol off the nightstand before pulling an extra clip from the drawer and stuffing it into my back pocket. Knowing it's a clear line-of-sight from the bedroom to the kitchen, I have no cover if I open the bedroom door.

My best chances are to take them from behind. Which also means I will leave Venecia unprotected until I make my way into the back of the cabin.

Looking out the window, I am unable to see anyone. Quietly flipping the latch, I slide it open and jump to the ground below. Quickly getting to my feet, I look around for any signs of men other than those I know are in the house. Unable to see any additional men, I stealthily make my way around the house.

I need to get to them before they get to the bedroom...before they get to her.

Pausing to look around the corner, there is one guy standing at the rear door. Taking advantage of the fact that his attention is focused on the men currently making their way through the house, I silently sneak up behind him. In a solitary movement, I wrap my hand over his mouth and slide the knife through his throat, ensuring he doesn't have the opportunity to make a sound as I kill him. Holding him tightly, his blood flows down my arm as I quietly lower him to the ground trying not to alert the others.

Crossing the threshold, I see that there are two more men in the cabin – one just inside the bedroom door and the other several feet behind him in the living room. Traversing the kitchen, my breaths slow and steady, my bare feet enabling me to stay silent as I sneak up behind them.

They are so close to Venecia, I can't risk taking them one at time. The knife in my left hand and the Glock in my right, I creep behind them. Awkwardly shoving the knife into the lung of the man in front of me, I step around him and shoot the other with his hand on the knob of the closet door.

Venecia's screams overshadow the echo of the gun firing, as I pump two more rounds into him before returning my attention to the pissed off guy with the knife sticking from his side. Shoving the pistol into his chest, I fire three times before pulling the knife from him. His body immediately falling to the floor.

Stepping over him, I rush to the closet and shove the dead body on the floor out of the way.

I need to get to her.

"It's me, *cuore mio*," turning the knob I pull the closet open to find the barrel of the gun shaking in my face, "It's me."

Still trembling her hands slightly lower the gun before I take it from her hands and pull her into my arms. Her body trembles against me as she cries.

VENECIA

"You're okay," Dante holds me tight against his body and I sob against his bare chest.

When the gun shots started firing, the only thought I had was that Dante was dead...and that I would be next.

His large hand brushes the hair from my face before his rough hands wipe the tears from my face, "I know you're scared, but we have to go."

Fighting back more tears, his lips press to my forehead. Lingering close to my face after the kiss, "Can you get dressed and grab your things?"

I nod my head as he continues to wipe the tears from my eyes.

Fumbling through the drawers and the closet, my primary focus is keeping my eyes off the two guys lying motionless on the floor, as I quickly throw on a pair of shorts and one of Dante's t-shirts. Once dressed, I haphazardly start shoving the rest of my things into my suitcase.

Dante has dropped two duffel bags by the front door. Based on the sound of cabinet doors opening and closing, he is gathering some necessities from the kitchen. I am still emptying out a drawer when he drops the box of things he's collected by the front door.

"Let me help you," his hands slide over mine in the drawer as he takes the clothes from my grip before quickly shoving them into my suitcase. Within seconds he has everything packed and is bending to zip it shut.

His shirt lifts as he bends, and a shudder runs through me when my eyes glimpse the guns tucked into the back of his jeans. It feels as though every terrifying emotion I felt in the closet just ran down my spine.

"Come on," Dante raps his arm around my back, "It's okay now. You're safe. You are safe with me. You will always be safe with me, but we have to get out of here."

Leading me from the bedroom, he loads his arms with the duffle bags and box by the door before heading towards the car. After putting everything in the back of the SUV, Dante pulls open the passenger door. With his hands wrapped around my waist, he helps lift me into passenger seat. Pulling the seatbelt around my body, his lips graze over mine while he buckles me in.

He quickly climbs into the driver's seat, turns over the engine, and accelerates down a dirt road running along the lake. My fingers are gripped so tightly around the door handle that my knuckles are turning white. My heart is still racing from the attack on the cabin...and also the speeds at which Dante is driving through these woods.

"I need you to write down the numbers in my phone," he pushes his cell phone into my hand, "There should be a pen in the glove box."

"Okay," I release my grip on the handle, "But why?"

"I will answer all of your questions later, but right now, *cuore mio*, I just need you to listen. Write down the numbers, please."

Grabbing a piece of paper and the pen from the glove box I scribble down phone numbers for Papa, Renzo, and Carlo – none of them numbers I am familiar with – before writing down those for a few other guys that work for the family.

"Good," Dante nods approvingly when I finish, "Now throw it out the window."

My shaky finger presses the button to crack the window and I slide the phone through the gap before rolling the window back up.

As I am tucking the paper into my pocket, Dante pulls the Tahoe to a stop in front of a rundown repair shop.

"Wait here," Dante opens his door and disappears behind the shop. A few minutes later a rusted Chevy, that looks to be older than me, pulls up behind the SUV and Dante climbs out. He pops the trunk on the car before coming to my door.

"Get in the car," he helps me from the SUV and tosses the keys onto the driver's seat, "I just need to move our things."

My hands are still shaking as I climb into the car. I may have grown up as the daughter to one of the city's most ruthless crime bosses, but until today not once have I ever been subjected to this side of things. Papa has always ensured he sheltered me from being in the company of violence and death.

From the moment he climbed into the car, Dante's hand has been on my thigh, his grip gentle yet comforting. Other than the occasional rattling noises coming from the engine, the ride is near silent.

Chapter Twenty

DANTE

As much as I want to tell Venecia what is going on, my entire focus is getting her somewhere safe first. And I know what I need to tell her can't be done while we are driving down the highway. Unable to bring myself to make small talk, we ride in silence, my hand gently squeezing her thigh in a poor attempt at comforting her.

We are just outside Binghamton when I pull into the parking lot of a small diner. Pulling towards the back corner, I back into a spot that will provide us with a little bit of privacy and ensure a quick getaway in the event it is needed.

Turning towards Venecia, the moment she realizes she has my undivided attention, she blurts out,

"What the fuck is going on?" before I have a chance to speak.

"I'm going to tell you everything," I cup her scared face in my hands, "I had to get you somewhere safe first."

"I thought you had me somewhere safe," she spits back.

"I did too," my head dips a little in shame for the danger she was in merely an hour ago, "I don't know how they found us.

The only things I can think of are the GPS and my phone, which is why we've ditched them both."

"What aren't you telling me? What happened last night?"

"Sal and your brothers made it home safely," I pause while her body relaxes at knowing her family is safe, "All of them had text me last night, but when they returned home the house had been hit."

A small gasp escapes her lips, as tries to process the shock of someone having the audacity to attack the Botticellis in their home.

"They took out all of the guards," I carefully choose my next words, "and Avalie has been taken."

"Who has her? What do they want?" the questions continue to rattle from her until she realizes what we both know this means.

Lorenzo is going to burn down the city to get her back.

"Fuck," her hand clamps over her mouth as she whimpers, "my family."

Unbuckling her seatbelt, I pull her across the seat to my lap and hold her against my chest.

"As much I wish I could, I can't answer all of your questions, *cuore mio*," my fingers tuck her hair behind her ear before drawing her face up to mine, "I only had time to read a few text messages before everything happened at the cabin. In those messages, Sal was clear that I keep you safe, and I intend to do just that."

Bridging the little bit of distance between us, my lips press against hers. Although usually every touch of her makes me want to devour her, this one is different – I just want her to know that I am here to take care of her.

With her on my lap, I hold her against my chest, petting her hair as we continue to talk and I try to comfort her. After a while, the tenseness in her body relaxes a little and the thumping of her heart begins to slow.

"There is a drug store across the street," I motion to the little pharmacy, "We need to grab a new burner phone and then we can get some breakfast before we disappear for a few days."

Opening the door, I help her slide off my lap before climbing from the car myself. Popping the trunk, I pull a several hundred dollars in small bills from one of the bags.

Taking her hand into mine, we walk across the street to the pharmacy. Being outside of my arms and surrounded by people, she is suddenly so tense; it nearly looks as those I am holding her against her will.

"You're going to need to relax and act natural," I squeeze her hand, "we're just a couple running errands and grabbing breakfast. We don't want to look like we're on the run."

VENECIA

"Relax? Easy for you to say," I scoff back at him trying to push out a small smile, "Some of us aren't used to gunshots and dead bodies before our morning coffee."

"There's my girl," he squeezes my hand again before leading me into the store.

Walking along the end caps of the aisles, Dante quickly finds the area with prepaid phones. Pulling one from the shelf and grabbing a card that matches the box, we get in line to pay. After a quick scan of our items, Dante pays in cash and we are on our way across the street to the diner.

"Welcome," an older woman in a retro-styled waitress uniform approaches us, "Just the two of ya this morning?"

"Yes, ma'am," Dante flashes back a ridiculous smile at her, "Would you mind if we took that booth in the back corner?"

"Help yourselves," she gestures towards the booth, "coffees?"

"Yes, please."

With his hand on the small of my back, Dante leads me toward the booth and gestures for me to slide into the bench against the wall before sliding in next to me. Once sitting, it dawns on me why he requested this booth - we can see every inch of the diner from here.

Opening the phone box, he inserts the battery, and types a bunch of numbers from the card into the phone, "The phone numbers?"

Pulling the list of numbers from my pocket, he keys in the one I had listed for Papa as the waitress brings our coffees to the table.

"Are we eating this morning," she smiles adoringly at the two of us sharing the one side of the booth and sitting so close to each other, "or just the coffees?"

"Definitely eating," Dante replies to her, "Can I get a pork roll sandwich? And she'll have the pancakes."

While he doesn't look at me, I can hear the amusement in his voice as he continues, "And she's going to need extra syrup with those."

My cheeks are warming and I am certain that my entire face is currently the color of a tomato when the waitress moves her attention to me.

"Bit of a sweet tooth," she chuckles at me, "Me too, honey."

Dante laughs quietly to himself as the waitress walks away from the table, "I thought you liked syrup."

Getting back to the phone, he pulls up the text message again and types to Papa.

> DANTE
> New number. Cabin was hit, needs clean up
>
> She is unharmed.

> SAL
> Bless you. All good?

> DANTE
> Going off grid for a few days
>
> No phone. No GPS.
>
> That has to be how they found us

> SAL
> Keep her safe.

Venecia whispers, "Tell him I want all of them to be safe."

DANTE

Keep yourselves safe for her.

He presses the power button and pulls the battery from the back of the flip phone. As he's shoving them into his back pocket, the waitress brings our breakfast to the table. The pancakes she places in front of me on the table have five little plastic tubs of syrup wedged up against them.

"Is that going to be enough syrup dear?" she questions.

This poor woman watches me, with no idea why my face is suddenly turning bright red again, "Yes. This will be more than enough."

"I'm never going to be able to eat pancakes without blushing ever again," I mumble as she walks away from the table.

"Good," Dante's fingers wrap underneath my chin and he pulls me in for a soft, gentle kiss.

His lips just parted from mine, he whispers, "I like seeing what thinking of my tongue on your body does to you."

Chapter Twenty-One

DANTE

After finishing up breakfast, we get back in the car and on the highway, talking openly about what is likely going to happen next back home. The only reassurance I really have that her family will be okay is that they are a bunch of tough motherfuckers.

Knowing that we need to go somewhere we can blend in and hide away, I drive us into the city of Binghamton. We drive aimlessly around the city until I find what it is that I am looking for.

The area of the city we are in is the opposite of the glamorous surroundings Venecia grew up in. Homes here are small, run down, and vastly outnumbered by less than luxurious apartment buildings. There are more boarded up businesses than there are ones with open doors.

Flipping on the blinker, I pull into a rundown two-story motel. While some of the people staying here might be travelers on a very tight budget, this is the type of place that many people down on their luck call home.

The similarities this place has to my home as a child are uncanny.

"Here," Venecia looks out the window, "We have plenty of cash to stay somewhere just a little bit nicer."

"We do," I pull into a parking spot, "but those kinds of places require credit cards and IDs. Wait here. Lock the doors. I'm going to go get us a room for the week."

Walking into the office, I find a portly man watching television behind the counter. He barely looks up to acknowledge me, "Sixty per night or two fifty for the week. Long term also require a fifty dollar deposit."

"I'll take the week," I pull three hundred dollars from my pocket and place it on the counter, "I'll let you know in a few days if I need longer."

The disheveled man stands and grabs a key from the board behind him before swiping my money off the counter. Dropping the key on the counter in front of me, "No drugs. No whores. I don't tolerate any trouble around here. The dumpster is around back and housekeeping is on Monday.

On the outside my face is acknowledging everything this man says, but on the inside I'm wonder what the fuck he's going to do to stop me from doing whatever the fuck I want.

Not that I have an intention of drugs, whores, or creating a problem.

"Got it," I pick up the keys, "You don't by chance have a trash bag laying around, do you?"

"One dollar."

Pulling the dollar from my pocket, I extend my hand to him while he grabs a trash bag out of a jumbo-sized Great Value box.

That whole fucking box probably only cost him ten dollars.

"Thanks,"

I take the bag from him and head back out to the car. When I approach her door, Venecia pushes the button to unlock the doors. Opening her door, I help her out of the car and lead her towards the trunk. Popping it open, I pull out my duffel bags and drop them on the ground before unzipping her suitcase.

"What are you doing," she questions as I begin to shove all her belongings into the trash bag.

"*Cuore mio*. If anyone watches me carry this Louis Vuitton bag into our room, we're going to be looking to get robbed the second the sun goes down."

Closing the trunk, I grab our belongings, "Walk behind me. Stay close. Keep your eyes on the ground. No matter what. Understand?"

"Yes," she mumbles as we begin walking towards the room. The walkway is littered with trash, a few scattered needles, and an occasional abandoned toy.

Putting the key in the door, I jimmy the handle to get it to turn. Finally getting it unlocked, I open the door, and motion for Venecia to enter the room first.

Yup. Just like home.

VENECIA

It doesn't take long to glance around the room. Even with as tiny as it is, it is the barest hotel room I have ever been in.

Just inside the door is a small wooden table with two mismatched diner style chairs. They nearly butt up to the sole nightstand, which is also wedged tightly against the queen-sized bed pressed into the far corner of the room. At the foot of the bed is a small dresser with a tiny tube television on top, leaving barely enough room to pass between them. Next to it hangs a cheap floor-length mirror.

Beyond that, there is nothing on the walls, except an occasional piece of tape holding the wallpaper to the wall and the dusty curtains hanging over the window.

The only door at the far side of the room must be the bathroom.

"I know it's not what you're used to," Dante drops the bags against the door to outside, "but we'll be safe here."

"Seriously?"

"Yes. While this is a shithole, it is also the type of place where everyone minds their own business," he pauses while he crosses the distance between us, "People don't ask questions, and they don't talk."

Leading me towards the bed, he sits against the headboard and pulls my body between his legs. Laying between his legs, my back against his chest, his arms slowly wrap around me.

"How do you know that?"

"After my dad died, I grew up in a place not too different from this one until my mom met Tony and remarried," his voice is soft and carrying just a tinge of embarrassment, "Everyone keeps to themselves.

They are so focused on surviving, they don't have time to worry about, or care, what their neighbors are doing."

Wrapping my hands over his arms, "You didn't tell me that. When you talked about your mom and growing up, it all sounded so happy."

"Part of it was," his arms tighten around me, "and that's the part I like to remember. We bounced around trash motels a lot, but she did the best she could with the cards she was dealt. She sheltered me from it for a long time and did whatever she could to make sure I was taken care of."

"She sounds like a wonderful woman. I wish I could have met her."

"I wish she could have met you," his hand lifts my face towards his, "she would have loved you."

"What makes you say that?"

"Because you are an amazing woman. But mostly, because, *cuore* mio, I love you."

Pressing my face up to his, his lips melt into mine. The kiss and his words tingle throughout my body.

Parting my lips, his tongue slowly enters my mouth and softly dances with my mine.

Releasing his grip on me, his hands grab my shirt and pull it over my head interrupting our kiss. Reaching between us, his fingers quickly unhook my bra before slowly sliding it down my arms. With his lips on my neck, his hands delicately rub over my stomach and up to my breasts. My back arches against his chest as he continues to gently caress me with his lips and hands.

"Take off your shorts and panties," his lips whisper against my ear.

Doing as he asks, I lift my butt from the bed and slide my remaining clothes down my legs and over my feet before dropping them next to us on the bed.

His hands reach under my thighs, and he lifts, positioning my feet on the bed outside of his straddled legs.

"Do you see how fucking wet you are for me?" his hands slide from my knees down my inner thighs, "Look in the mirror and watch how your perfect little pussy drips for my touch."

My eyes glance at the mirror hanging just past the foot of the bed, and I immediately turn my face away, embarrassed at seeing myself on full display from the way he positioned me.

"No, *cuore mio*," his left hand grabs my chin and turns my face back to the mirror, "I want you to watch as I make you come."

Holding my chin in place, I watch as his right hand gently twists and pulls at my nipple causing my hips to flex as I chew on my lower lip. His hand slowly rubs over my entrance until his fingers are wet with my arousal before sliding them over my clit. My eyes close as I arch against his touch.

"Eyes on the mirror," the hand on my chin slides down my neck and his fingers wrap tightly around my throat, "Watch how beautifully you come for me."

His fingers expertly play with my clit, bringing me quickly to the edge. Keeping my eyes on the mirror is hard. Watching myself feels dirty and wrong.

But it is fucking hot.

I can't even try to argue how much it turns me on, as I watch my arousal slowly soak the blankets beneath me.

The orgasm consumes my body, and I come with a power I didn't know was possible. My eyes stay fixed on the mirror watching my body quiver and explode as he makes me come.

"You're fucking beautiful," his fingers continue to play between my legs, urging another orgasm from me, "aren't you?"

"Yes," a raspy moan rattles from my chest as he pushes me over the edge.

"Two more," his grip tightens around my throat and the fingers between my thighs pick up speed, "and then you can watch how well you take my cock."

Chapter Twenty-Two

DANTE

It only takes a moment before her body is writhing against me as her third orgasm consumes her. Her eyes stay focused on her reflection in the mirror, and she watches herself with lusty, hooded eyes.

"Get on your hands and knees," I slide from under her as she begins to move. As she gets into position, I stand from the bed and remove my pants, "Put that beautiful ass in the air for me."

Climbing onto the bed, I settle behind her perky ass and press the tip of my throbbing erection to her dripping entrance, "Eyes on the mirror. Watch as you take my cock, as I slide it inside of you."

Gently holding her hips, I watch her face in the mirror as I slowly slide every inch of me inside her soaked cunt. She is fucking beautiful, as she struggles against the pleasure to keep her eyes open, while I slowly stretch and fill her. I draw myself back out of her and begin steadily thrusting into her.

When her whimpers become louder and her hips begin pushing back to meet mine, my fingers tighten their grip and I pick up a punishing pace.

"Watch how my cock makes you come," I growl through my thrusts, "how much you fucking love how it makes you feel."

Screams leave her mouth as she spasms tightly around my cock, yet she keeps her eyes open as she continues watch herself come completely undone.

By the time she rides out the orgasm, she is exhausted and struggling to hold her body up.

Reaching around her, I lift her body so that her back is once again against my chest. Slowly thrusting into her, my lips against her ear, I whisper, "Such a good fucking girl." Holding her against me, her body trembles with every thrust of my cock, "Can my good girl handle one more?"

With heavy eyes, she nods in response to my question. "Good," my lips roam her neck as my fingers linger over her sensitive clit, "because I want to fill you with my cum so that we can watch it drip from you."

"Dante...," her raspy voice carries a tinge of concern and I know it's because we are rolling the dice not using any form of contraception.

I moan back into her ear, "*Cuore mio*, I want everything that comes from finishing buried deep inside of you. But if you tell me to pull out, I will."

"Dante...," tears well in her eyes while her heavy head falls back on my shoulder, my cock continuing to rock in and out of her while my fingers play with her clit. Her hips ride mine, only further drawing my release from me.

When her body tightens and she clamps hard around my cock, I am unable to hold back any longer. With a loud groan in her ear, I empty myself inside of her, not stopping until she has milked every drop of cum from me.

With my cock still buried deep inside, and my arms tightly wrapped around her, I rest her on my thighs and hold her exhausted body against mine. Gradually going soft inside of her, my cum begins to slowly trickle down her thighs.

"Do you see how fucking beautiful we are together?" I watch as her fingers glide through the cum on her thigh. I groan watching her bring my collected release to her mouth and sucking it from her fingers.

When she is done cleaning me from her thighs, I lay our bodies onto the bed with my arms wrapped around her chest, "You're fucking beautiful. So fucking perfect."

We lay in silence. The only sounds in this room our breaths and the occasional rattle of the air conditioner. Just when I think she has fallen asleep, she whispers, "Dante?"

"Yes, *cuore mio*?"

"I love you too.

VENECIA

"I love you too," the words flow from my mouth without hesitation.

Considering the fact that I have never spoken those words to anyone but my family, I would have thought that it would feel weird to say them. But it wasn't. Instead it felt complete natural, as though I have been saying it to him my whole life.

My face resting on his sweaty chest, my hair damp from my own exertion draped across us, "Did you mean it?"

"Did I mean what?"

"What you said about finishing inside of me?"

Tilting my face towards his, I see his angling down towards mine and kissing my forehead, "Of course, *cuore mio*."

It's ridiculous.

Crazy, even.

And I know that logically the idea of possibly getting pregnant is insane.

Maybe I'm sex drunk. Maybe I'm in some weird euphoria from hearing that he loves me.

Fuck, maybe it's some crazy trauma response to thinking I was going to die this morning.

All I know is that I like the idea of growing his children inside of me.

As much as I want to tell him, to talk about this, my physical exhaustion from how far he continues to push my body gets the better of me. Within minutes the repetitive thump of his heart has me drifting off to sleep in the comfort of his arms.

* * *

The next three days are spent confined to this motel room – talking, eating take-out, and watching old reruns on the grainy TV.

It's mid-afternoon when Dante pulls the disposable phone from his bag and slides the battery into the back. Powering it on, it takes a moment for it to connect to service. When it does, two text messages from yesterday ding through.

SAL

Everyone is home

Come join us

DANTE

Great news sir

We'll be there late tonight

SAL

Looking forward to it

Chapter Twenty-Three

VENECIA

"Time to head home, I guess," Dante drops the cell phone back into his bag.

As excited as I am to hear those words and see my family, my stomach drops at the same time. My face must fall too, because there is an immediate look on concern on Dante's.

"What's wrong, *cuore mio*?" his hands cup my face.

"This," I feel the tears welling in my eyes and I try to fight them, "I can't go back to how it was. Back to there being nothing being us."

His large hands squeeze my face as he pulls me in for a slow and sensual kiss. When he pulls back, his lips stay close enough that I can almost still feel them on mine.

"I love you, *cuore mio*," his eyes burn through to my soul and a tear rolls down my cheek, "You are mine. There will **never** be nothing between us."

As I press my body against him, his large arms envelope my body.

"You know my family will never accept this."

"If I have to, I will love you in private, until we figure out how to tell your family. But we will tell your family."

"They'll kill you," I quietly sob into his chest.

"That's a risk I am more than willing to take for you," his arms hold me tighter, "but they would never, when they realize that it would kill you too."

Quietly we pack up our belongings and Dante carries them all to the car. Walking from the motel, I look back towards our room.

I can't believe that I'm actually going to miss this shithole.

The ride back to the city is nearly six hours, and most of it is spent in silence. The only comfort I have right now is the words he spoke to me, knowing he wants to grow a family with me, and his warm hand on my thigh. It feels like my world is imploding and I don't know how to sit here and have a conversation when I feel like I'm dying. Based on Dante's lack of conversation, I can only assume he feels the same.

When we are a few miles from home, Dante pulls the car onto a side street and parks against the curb.

"I need to kiss you one more time," he unbuckles my seatbelt and pulls me onto his lap so that I am straddling him, "before I can no longer touch your lips whenever I want."

His fingers rake up my back and into my hair, as he grips it tightly and pulls my face into his. His mouth devours mine. This kiss is hard and needy, yet he savors it as though it is his final meal before execution. It almost feels as though he will never get to kiss me again. His teeth gently pull on my lower lip when our faces separate, both of us left red and breathless.

Releasing my hair, his fingers retreat down my spine before his hands settle around my waist. Lifting me from his lap, he places me back on the seat, waits for me to buckle my seatbelt and puts the car back in drive.

Both of his hands are on the wheel as we approach the estate a few minutes later. Pulling through the gate, I am again happy and crushed at the idea of returning home.

Papa is waiting on the steps as Dante pulls the car toward the house. The moment the car is parked, his hands are on the handle opening the door for me.

"Venecia," his hand lowers to help me out of the car. I take it, glancing back at Dante for a brief second, before stepping from the car.

"It's good to have my princess back home," Papa pulls me in for a tight hug.

Hugging him back, my heart aches, consumed with both happiness and sorrow, "It's good to be back home."

"I'm going to spend some time with my little girl," he addresses Dante, "but I want to speak with you later and thank you properly for taking care of her."

"My things," I sputter as I'm led into the house.

"Dante will bring your things up to your room."

DANTE

As Sal leads her inside, I am suddenly thrust back into the role of the hired help. Doing as Sal wanted, I unload our things from the car and carry them inside, stopping at the door to ask the guards if they could get someone to dispose of the rusted Chevy.

Dropping some of the bags in the foyer, I carry our things upstairs and place them in our respective rooms. Quickly heading back downstairs, I grab the remaining duffle bags and carry them back to the armory. Taking my time, I unpack them, unload, and meticulously clean the guns as I put everything back in its place.

As I am putting the last Glock away, Sal enters the room and approaches me with his hand reached out towards me. Extending mine in return, he shakes it while thanking me for taking care of his little girl.

I just want to tell him that I would do anything for her, including give my life to keep her safe.

Instead, I take his gratitude while acknowledging it is the job that he hired me for.

"It's late," Sal retreats towards the door, "We can talk tomorrow about what you would like to do next."

"Next?" the question blurts out of my mouth probably a little faster than it should.

"You have obviously proven your worth to this family. We need to discuss how to utilize you going forward," his hand taps the doorframe as he leaves the room.

Fuck. I hadn't thought of the possibility of being removed as her security.

Heading upstairs to get some sleep, my brain is reeling with ways to convince Sal to keep me where I am. My heart on the other hand is terrified that I will no longer have a reason to be around her.

Reaching my room, Venecia's door is closed. I hesitate for just a second to knock on it, before making the smart decision and heading into my own. After kicking off my shoes and stripping out of my clothes, I climb into the bed.

It feels massive and empty without her tiny body being pressed up against mine.

Most of the night is spent thinking about how either of us will survive if I am removed from her security. The rest is spent missing the feel of her naked body nuzzled tightly against mine. It isn't until the early hours of the morning that I manage to fall asleep.

Waking a few hours later, I am showered and dressed by seven, and heading down to the kitchen to get a cup of coffee. While I am a little surprised to see her, her schedule has changed dramatically in the past few days. Venecia is standing at the coffee pot, with her back to me, waiting for it to finish brewing. Walking towards the coffee pot, my eyes are completely fixated on the tiny bit of ass peaking from the bottom of her shorts.

"Good morning, *cuore mio*," I whisper as I approach behind her, prompting her to spin around. When she turns, I am met with a blushing smile.

"Morning, Dante," she glances over my shoulder and smiles, "Morning, Papa."

"Since when do you get up this early in the morning," he calls across the kitchen.

"Dante wasn't big on letting me sleep in," the corner of her mouth ticks as she tries to hide her smile, the two of us secretly aware that most mornings I would wake her with my face buried between her thighs.

Chapter Twenty-Four

DANTE

"I was going to wait until a little later in the day," Sal looks to me, "but since you're up and we're both free, why don't we take our coffee to my office and finish our conversation from last night."

"Of course, sir."

Following him down the hall to his office, I push the door shut behind us and take a seat opposite him at the desk.

"Did you give any thought to what I said last night," he takes a sip of his coffee, "and what it is that you would like to do with the family going forward? If not, I have some ideas as to where your skills would be a good fit."

"Actually, sir," I try to ensure my voice sounds pragmatic, "I think it would be best if I stayed on with Venecia for a little while longer."

Taking a brief sip of my coffee, I watch as Sal slightly arches an inquisitive eyebrow, "With all that has happened and how uncertain things still are, I think it is in her best interest to have someone protecting her when she leaves this house."

It feels like an eternity that Sal stares back at me before he speaks, "While she is one of the most important things in the world to me, after all you did to keep her safe, I didn't want you to feel like you were going to be stuck babysitting her."

"It's not babysitting, sir," I politely retort, "It took us a while to get on the same page about things, but I'd like to see this out until it you know it is safe for her again."

"Good man, Dante," he nods approvingly at my response, "Get one of the boys the address to the cabin. We'll get some cleaners up there ASAP to take care of things."

"I appreciate that."

"It's the least I can do for taking care of her."

If you only knew how I was actually taking care of her, this would be an entirely different conversation.

"You are welcome, and encouraged, to stay here while you continue to protect her."

"Of course," I nod back while extending my hand over the desk to shake his hand.

Grabbing my coffee, I return to the kitchen, but Venecia is no longer in there. After rinsing my cup and leaving it in the sink, I head upstairs to my room to unpack the bag I didn't get to last night.

Opening the door, I am surprised to be greeted by Venecia in nothing but a sheer, black, strappy thong, matching bra, and stilettos. Quickly stepping inside, I scramble to shut and lock the door before anyone sees her in here like this.

"Are you fucking crazy?" I smirk at her.

"I missed having your arms around me while I slept last night," her hands graze over her stomach before rubbing over her panties, "and I definitely missed having my alarm clock in bed with me this morning."

"You know we can't do this here."

"No, I know we shouldn't," her hand grips my firm cock through my pants, "but it's quite obvious we both want to."

She lowers herself to her knees, unbuttons my pants and pulls them down until she frees my cock. Looking up at me, she opens her mouth and slowly swallows me to the base.

Fuck, she's gotten good at this.

My hands gather her hair and hold it in a ponytail as she continues to slide my cock in and out of her throat.

"*Cuore mio,*" I groan as her tongue swirls around my tip.

VENECIA

Using the grip of my hair, Dante pulls himself from my mouth before helping me to my feet. Taking my mouth, his fingers pull my panties to the side and he slides them inside of me.

"My little whore likes sucking cock," his fingers pump in and out of me, "you get so fucking wet with my cock deep in your throat."

Gripping my thighs, he lifts me from the floor. My legs wrapping around his waist as he slides himself inside of me.

"Fuck," I moan quietly when he bottoms out inside of me.

"Shhhh," he whispers into my ear as he continues move my body up and down his cock. Working me over him, my legs rhythmically squeeze his waist trying to make him take me faster.

"Is this not enough?" he quickly drops me down over his cock, "Does my little whore need more?"

"Yes," I groan as he impales me again, slamming my back against the wall before he begins vigorously thrusting into me.

My back arches and I bury my face in his neck, trying to muffle my screams as I feel the release I needed building at my core.

"Right there," he changes the angle of his thrusts and I can't hold it back any longer.

My fingers tear through the flesh on his back as the orgasm explodes through me, "Oh my god, just like tha-"

His free hand clamps over my mouth silencing my screams.

"Shhh, *cuore mio*," the words a deep whisper in my ear, "I love to make you scream for me, but someone will hear us."

His words tell me to be quiet, but the relentless thrusts of his cock repeatedly slamming me against the wall tell me he wants someone to find us.

He quietly groans in my ear as I squeeze around his cock, rocking my hips, when I come again.

Lowering me to the ground, he drops to his knees in front of me. Grabbing the strings of my panties, he slides them down my legs until I need to step from them.

I expect him to toss them to the floor, but he rubs them over my entrance before reaching up and putting them in my hand. They are soaked through with my arousal.

"Put them in your mouth," he growls, staring up at me as he throws one of my legs over his shoulder, "I'm not asking. In your mouth. Now."

Balling them up, I open my lips and hesitantly press them into my mouth. The tangy sweetness of my own arousal immediately hits my tongue.

"Such a good little whore," his tongue flicks over my clit, "Now be quiet while I reward you for listening so well."

Gripping my ass with both hands, he buries his face between my thighs. His tongue and teeth are violent in their assault on my clit, and I am fervently riding his face chasing my next orgasm. When it hits, I scream out, but it is muffled by the wet panties shoved in my mouth.

Sucking on my clit, Dante slides my trembling leg from his shoulder and sets my foot back on the ground. His tongue dips inside my entrance and up the length of my slit before he stands in front of me.

His fingers slide between my lips and pull the panties from my mouth, before he replaces them with his tongue. His tongue pushing his mouthful of his saliva and my arousal into my mouth.

"Does my good little whore like the taste of her cunt?" his fingers wrap around my throat as begin to firmly squeeze..

I struggle to swallow with his tight grip on my neck, before responding, "Yes."

"Good," the hand around my throat pushes me back down to my knees, "because I want you to clean yourself from my cock before I come down your throat."

Chapter Twenty-Five

DANTE

We have been sneaking around this house for nearly a month. It is a miracle that we haven't been caught yet.

Pulling on my sneakers, I head downstairs to take my daily sunrise run around the massive property. Venecia is at the bottom of the stairs, wearing a tiny pair of running shorts, a sports bra that zips down the front, and her sneakers. She stands from her stretch to see me on the stairs, "You're late, sleepyhead."

It is also a miracle that no one has caught on to what actually happens on these morning runs.

We head out the door and begin jogging down the driveway before veering off towards a trail that leads into the woods. She is in front of me, granting me a remarkable view of her bouncing ass, as she runs.

"You better fucking run, *cuore mio*," I call out from behind her, "because when I catch you, I intend to take what I want from your body."

She picks up her pace and turns down one of the trails that run deeper in the woods surrounding the property. Increasing my speed, I am nearly at a sprint as I begin to close the distance between us. Reaching her, she squeals, when my arm wraps around her waist and lift her from the ground.

Holding her against me, she giggles and screams out for help as my hand undoes the zipper on her sports bra, freeing her heaving breasts. My hands playing with both of her nipples, as I lower us both to the ground before laying my body on top of hers. Reaching between us, I yank her shorts down to her thighs and push mine underneath my throbbing cock.

As much as I enjoy making her beg, there isn't time for that out here in the open. Lifting her hips slightly, she screams out as I shove the entirety of my length inside her. Our knees both dig into the ground as I continue to pound into her. She cries out as she comes, and I empty myself inside of her before pulling out.

My fingers trail through the cum that spills out onto her thighs before pressing them between the cheeks of her ass. Her body pressing back against them, always wanting more.

"I plan to fill this this hole with my cum soon," airy mewls pass her lips as I firmly rub it over and around her tight little hole.

The thought of my cock in her tight little ass has me growing hard again. Stroking my length a few times, I press back into her cunt already dripping with my cum.

Taking her rough and hard for the second time, I cover my hand over her mouth trying to silence her faux screams for help mixed with her screams of pleasure.

"What the fuck," a male voice yells from behind me. I hear feet quickly treading towards us. Turning my head, I am met with a fist before being yanked off Venecia. Thrown to the ground, the body is immediately on top of me railing me with brutal punches to the face.

"Who the fuck do you think you are," spittle hits my face with his fist, "thinking you could rape my sister and get away with it."

"I didn't," I sputter, lifting my hands to protect myself.

"The fuck you didn't," he hits me again, "I fucking heard her screaming."

The last things I hear are Venecia screaming for him to stop and his fist breaking my nose.

VENECIA

Although I don't make out the words, my body jumps when I hear a man yelling from the woods. Dante is ripped from inside of me, leaving me exposed on the ground. Scrambling to cover myself, I pull my shorts over my ass and use my hands to hold my bra together as I fumble with the zipper.

By the time I stand up, Renzo is straddling Dante and throwing repeated punches to his face. He is already a bloody mess.

"Stop," the words shrill scream as I run towards them, "Renzo, stop!"

Just as I reach them, Renzo throws another punch. The cracking of bone in Dante's face echoes through the trees around us, and his body goes limp.

Climbing off him, Renzo grabs the front of his shirt and lifts his upper body from the ground as he begins dragging him back to the house.

He's going to fucking kill him.

"Renzo," I continue to yell as his drags the near-lifeless body up to the house, "Stop! It's not what you think! Renzo!"

We are apparently making quite the commotion, because Papa, Ava and Luca are coming down the stairs as we approach.

"What the fuck is going on?" Papa yells while quickly walking towards us.

"This fucking piece of shit had V pinned to the ground in the middle of the woods," Renzo spits back angrily.

"That's not what happened," I cry out as they drag his body up the stairs, "I mean, that is what happened, but..."

"Luca," Papa yells up to the stairs, "help Renzo get him to the basement."

His eyes look over me, and I realize that I am covered in dirt and have tears streaming down my face. My appearance pretty much substantiating Renzo's claims.

"Ava," he reaches for me, but I pull away, "Please take her upstairs and see that she is okay. You know the number to Doc."

Before I have a moment to protest, the guys have already disappeared into the house with Dante. Papa is not far behind them.

Ava walks towards me and gently reaches for my hand, "Come on V, let's get you inside and get you cleaned up."

I want to scream and make them all listen.

Words won't leave my mouth, completely overwhelmed it's like my brain just shuts down.

Instead, nothing comes out of me except for giant sobs.

"You're okay now," Ava leads me up the stairs, "We've all got you."

After leading me into the bathroom, Ava sits with me on the bathroom floor and holds me while I cry. She tries to comfort me but doesn't realize that in this moment all my fear is about what is happening to Dante, not what they all think happened to me.

While everything thinks I am naïve, I know very well what types of things happen in that basement. Men go down there. Not everyone comes back up.

My sobs subside as I slowly gain composure over myself. When she realizes I've stopped crying, Ava stands and helps me to my feet before turning on the shower, "Let's get some of this dirt washed off you."

Her eyes look over my body, taking in how dirty and disheveled I am. A small gasp leaves her mouth when her gaze reaches my thighs.

"Oh sweetheart," her eyes fixate on the cum both dried and dripping down my thighs, "It's okay. We'll call the doc and have him bring over a Plan B for you."

Peeling off my clothes, she forces me to step into the shower before I respond, "I can't take that."

"I know your family is Catholic-"

"No," I cut her off while I quickly scrub the dirt from my knees and elbows, "I can't take that because I'm already pregnant."

"I know the boys have kept you pretty sheltered, but that's not how it works."

"I'm not fucking stupid," I snicker back from inside the shower, leaning out to look at her, "I know how it works. Check the trash. I just found out this morning."

Ava is bent over the trash can as I am stepping out of the shower. I wrap the towel around my body while I watch her hand reach into the trash. When she stands, she is holding my positive test.

Chapter Twenty-Six

DANTE

My face is fucking killing me when I come to. The only thing that hurts more is the burning pain in my shoulders. It takes a moment, but I realize that my arms are bound above my head and my feet are barely dusting the floor.

Opening my eyes, I am met with Lorenzo, Sal, and Luca all sitting in chairs looking back at me. All of them have a murderous glint in their eyes as they stare at me, but it is Lorenzo aimlessly twirling the knife in his lap that has me the most concerned.

I have only heard stories about what he does with that knife down here.

"I brought you into this family," Sal shifts in his seat, "Into my home. And this is how you fucking repay my generosity?"

The butt of Lorenzo's knife jams into my gut when I open my mouth to speak, "You don't get to fucking talk unless we tell you to. Try it again and you'll be trying without a tongue."

His knife slices through each piece of my clothing until I am left dangling naked before them. The knife drags down my body stopping at the base of my cock, and Lorenzo presses the tip of the blade into my skin, "Test me, and you'll be lucky I don't cut your cock off to get things started."

Luca stands from his chair and walks behind me, while I can't see him, I am still more terrified of the man with the knife in front of me. As I should be. Luca merely holds me steady for Lorenzo to use as a punching bag. By the time he stops, his knuckles are bloody. I am splattered with his blood and all of my torso is red and already beginning to show the scattered with bruises.

He stops long enough to whisper something to Sal, before returning to me with a firm fist to my gut that momentarily takes my breath away. The moment I can suck in air, another fist hits me leaving me unable to breathe again. Even though it probably only lasts for a few minutes, this process repeats for what feels like hours.

My body is already exhausted, and if it were not for the bindings around my wrists my body would have collapsed to floor by now.

Luca spins me so that my back is to Lorenzo. Something jabs me hard in the kidney, yet again leaving me struggling to suck in air. I am breathless, and unable to cry out, when I feel the knife slide through the skin below my left shoulder blade.

"You want to disgrace our family...," his words dark and ruthless as the blade of the knife continues slicing through my skin.

I can feel the blood trickling down my back as he continues to carve into me.

"Then this family is going to disgrace you," his knife presses deep while he carves, and I feel everything slowly going black around me.

A hand slaps hard against my face, and I come to. As I open my eyes, Luca's hand slaps me again, "Morning, sunshine. Renzo's not done with you yet."

My face grimaces and I wince when the blade of the knife immediately pierces my skin again. This time it doesn't stop. He continues to carve into me, and the pain is nearly unbearable.

"B. O. T. T. I. C. E. L. L.," Lorenzo's fingers slowly trace over the knife marks he has left across my back.

The knife stabs deep and I cry out, "*Cuore mio*," as he drags it through both my skin and muscle to make the "I".

VENECIA

"What the fuck, V," she holds the test out to me, "How the fuck did you get pregnant?"

"You see," I smirk at her while walking towards the door, "When two people love each other very much."

"Very funny," she sarcastically snaps back at me, "You know what I mean. You aren't even seeing anyone."

"I've been seeing him for a little over a month," I push past her and walk into my room to get dressed.

"A little over a month ago you were locked away in the woods with Dante," I watch as her eyes go wide at the realization she just made, "Venecia? Tell me you weren't stupid enough to fuck your bodyguard."

"This," I pull on my shorts, "coming from the debt that's fucking my brother. I don't think you have room to be so judgmental."

"I love your brother."

"I love Dante," I pull the tank top over my still wet body.

"Truly," her tone changes as she questions me, "You truly love him."

"Yes," I nod back at her, "I was going to tell him this morning that we are going to have a baby, and then figure out how to tell the rest of you what the hell has been going on."

"It appears that second secret has already been spilled today," she grabs my hand as I step into the hallway, now pulling her behind me.

"I know Renzo," she squeezes my hand, "and if we don't hurry it might be too late."

"I know him too. Why the fuck do you think I'm heading downstairs?"

"We have to stop him before it's too late."

We practically drag each other down the stairs and to the basement door, where she enters the code into the keypad.

How the fuck does she know the code, no one is allowed down here.

Another time, this is better than my plan of banging on the door.

She pulls open the door, and I hear Dante call out in a pained voice, "*Cuore mio.*"

"Dante," I yell back as I take the stairs two at a time. I am unable to get to him fast enough, yet my legs freeze at the bottom of the stairs when I see his bloodied, naked body hanging on the far side of the room.

"Stop," I scream, and all their eyes turn to me, "What the fuck have you done to him?"

"We're taking care of it," Papa begins to walk towards me, "You don't have to worry about him."

"Go back upstairs," Renzo stalks back towards Dante, "You don't want to see this."

"Stop," I loudly cry, repeating myself while crossing the room towards them, "You need to stop!"

"Upstairs," Renzo roars back at me.

"Fellas," Ava calls from the stairs, "You fucking idiots need to listen to what she has to say."

In awe, I watch as all their jaws drop.

Apparently, her new-found lineage has granted her some clout, because I don't think I have ever heard anyone speak to either Papa or Renzo like that in my life. At least not anyone who lived to talk about it.

"Tell them," she walks with me towards all of them.

"Renzo. Whatever it is you think was happening in the woods is not what was happening."

"You're trying to tell me that he wasn't muffling your screams with his dick in you? I heard you screaming for help."

"That was happening, but it's not what you think," they all stare back at me in with some dumbfounded look, "I was a willing fucking participant. A more than willing participant, and I wasn't actually screaming for help you fucking idiot."

"What the fuck are you saying," Renzo shakes his head at me.

From beside me, I hear Ava chuckle, "Are you guys all that fucking dense? Does she really need to spell it out for you?"

"The woods wasn't the first time. I've been fucking him for over a month."

"Venecia," Papa hangs his head, "You don't know what you're talking about. He's nearly twice your age, and he obviously took advantage you."

Chapter Twenty-Seven

DANTE

"I would never take advantage of her!"

Luca shoves me, "What were you told about speaking out of turn?"

Venecia stalks towards him as though she is a six foot, three-hundred-pound man, and promptly shoves him back before grabbing a knife from the table, "Touch him again and you'll be the one not leaving this room. Understood?"

"Fuck, V," he puts his arms up in truce and backs away from us.

"I need all of you to listen to me," her voice firm, "I am not a little girl. While I appreciate the sentiment, all of you thinking that you are being righteous on my behalf, I don't need all of you to protect me like I am a child. He might be older than me, but he did not take advantage of me. He loves me too much to ever do anything to hurt me."

"Venecia," Sal sullenly interrupts her.

"No, Papa. I'm not done," she silences him, "I love him, and we are going to be together. If you don't like it, we don't have to stay here. But it'll be really fucking sad when you don't get to meet your first grandchild."

"His what," I groan through the pain when her words resonate.

Her eyes dart to Lorenzo, "Are you going to fucking cut him down? Or do I need to climb on a chair and do it myself?"

With a look of defeat and a smidge of disappointment, Lorenzo walks towards me with the knife and slices through the rope above my hands. My legs crumble below me, but Luca catches my body and gently lowers me to the floor. Venecia is immediately beside me on the floor untying the rope from my wrists, with watery eyes and a slight smile on her face.

"This conversation isn't over," Sal stands from his chair.

"No Papa, it is. The next conversation we have will be the three of you making your apologies to the father of my child."

"Fellas," Ava walks towards them, "You've all done enough. I think it's time we leave, and someone is going to need to be upstairs to let Doc down here."

As they all walk up the stairs, I use what little strength I have left to cup her face and pull her towards me and kiss her with everything I have.

"*Cuore mio*," I struggle to push out the words, "I love you...and our *bambino*."

My body falls into her lap, and she strokes my hair, "Just rest."

I don't remember much between falling asleep on her lap and waking up in her bed, with the exception a view vague moments of the doc stitching up some of the deeper cuts on my back and setting my nose back into place.

Everything hurts. My shoulders ache from holding the weight of my body. Every inch of my torso feels as though Lorenzo used me as a punching bag, and the sheets burn as they rub against the shallower cuts on my back not covered in bandages.

Yet, when I turn my head to find Venecia lying in bed beside me, I cannot help but smile.

"Good morning," she delicately straddles my hips and leans towards my face before kissing me. A groan releases into her mouth as she leans a little too hard against a tender spot on my ribs.

"I'm sorry," she pushes herself up.

Wrapping my arms around her, I pull her onto my body and kiss her back through the pain.

"Never apologize for loving me," I whisper against her lips.

VENECIA

Carefully rolling off Dante, I lay next to him in the bed and hold his hand.

"I will never apologize for loving you."

Dante winces as he rolls onto his side so that he is facing me, and I cannot help but rub my fingers over the extra scruff that has grown on his jaw.

"You've been pretty out of it for a little over two days," my fingers continue to trace delicately over his bruised jaw, "Doc had you pretty medicated to get you through the worst of things."

"Fuck," he groans with a hint of a smile, "This isn't the worst of it?"

After peppering soft kisses on his lips, I continue to fill him in on the things that happened while he was sleeping, "It took a bit for all of us to cool off, but I talked with Papa and Renzo last night. We can all be a little hot-headed and overreact sometimes."

I cannot help but snicker at the all-knowing face Dante makes back at me.

"I'm sorry," I squeeze his hand fighting back the urge to laugh inappropriately, "Things aren't good, but they're better."

"You mean no one is going to try to kill me when I leave this room?"

"Yeah," I smile back at him, "Renzo realizes that he fucked up and took things too far without actually knowing what was going on."

"Papa is still pretty hot that you had the nerve to deflower his precious little princess," I roll my eyes, "and he might take a little longer to fully come around, but he's working on it."

Sitting up on the bed, I gingerly climb over Dante and stand up on his side of the bed.

"I'm not saying things aren't going to be awkward as hell when you walk downstairs," I smile at him and reach my hands out to him, "but at least no one is going to try to kill you. I think. Now can we get you showered up because you kind of stink."

Chapter Twenty-Eight

DANTE

Venecia leads me to the bathroom and turns on the shower. Looking in the mirror as she steps behind me, I am met with my bruised face. I look like a man that went toe-to-toe with Lorenzo Botticelli.

"This might hurt a little," she picks at the surgical tape holding the bandages on my back to remove them.

A small hiss blows over my lips when part of the bandage sticks to the wound. In response, Venecia seethes, "That fucking asshole."

Turning my body to look at my back in the mirror, the Botticelli name spans the width of my shoulders and stands about five inches high.

"It hurt like fucking hell," I look back her, "but that's going to be sexy as fuck when it heals."

"What is wrong with you?"

"Absolutely nothing," I pull her into the shower.

"Are you sure aren't still high?"

"You are all a crazy bunch of motherfuckers," my hands pull her body flush against mine, "but I am proud to be branded as a Botticelli."

"You are still high," she smiles back and kisses me.

"And being one of the only men to survive your brother in the basement is going to give me one hell of a reputation."

"You're welcome for that," she smiles smugly.

"Have I mentioned yet how fucking hot you were down there? If I weren't in so much pain, I would've been hard as fucking hell for you," I pull her against my hard cock, "but now that I'm feeling better."

Gripping her face in my hands, I pull her up to my face before kissing her hard and deep. With every entanglement of my tongue with hers, it is apparent that I am kissing her as though I truly thought I would never get to kiss her again.

I cannot get enough of her. I need it. Need to prove to myself that I am still here with her.

Wincing slightly as I kneel to the shower floor before her, my hands slide down her body and stop on her stomach. Looking up at her, she smiles down at me and nods her head as though she knows I was questioning if that moment was real.

Kissing her stomach, I pull her leg over my shoulder and slide my tongue through her slit. Her hands grip my hair and pull me towards her.

VENECIA

His tongue licks over my clit and need more of him. I need to feel him again. I need him to relentlessly claim me.

Gripping his hair, I pull his face deeper between my thighs, while whimpering out a begging "Please."

He promptly gives me what I need, as he sucks, licks and gently bites at my clit. His tongue rubs firmly over my clit as I guide his head and rock my hips chasing my release. My hips quiver on his face and tongue as it builds at my center before passing through me with a scream.

Dante pulls his mouth from me and I look down to see him slowly stroking his cock as he slides two fingers inside of me. They gradually thrust in and out of me allowing me the opportunity to come down from my high. As I do, he begins to pick up speed and curling them towards him.

My hand fists his hair as my walls clench around his fingers and I come again.

"If you want my tongue again, *cuore mio,* show me."

My hand in his hair I pull him back between my legs and his tongue fervently licks at my clit as his fingers continue to work inside of me. Flexed on my toe, he holds most of my weight as I ride his face about to come again. His tongue stops and begins to suck violently on my clit while vigorously working his fingers.

"Fuck...Dante...," I scream, pulling his hair to drag his face from between my legs, as I come again.

Pulling against my grip in his hair, his lips wrap around my clit and he begins to suck again as his fingers quickly thrust in and out of me.

Just as I am about to come, he stops. Looking up at me he scowls, "Don't ever pull me from your sweet little cunt again. I'll be nice this time, but next time you will thoroughly pay for denying me what I want."

Returning his lips to my clit, he works diligently to bring me to the brink before stilling his fingers and pulling back from my clit.

He pulls my other leg over his shoulder before kissing my inner thighs, occasionally granting me one teasing lick or suck of my clit. My hips are writhing between his face and the wall.

"Dante....," I beg, "Please...."

His eyes look up at me as he continues kissing my thighs and teasing my clit.

"Please let me come," I plead with him.

The look in his eyes is feral at my words, and his tongue is lapping at my clit while his fingers plunge inside of me. My thighs flex against his face as I scream out my release. In turn, he begins to suck on my clit and curl his fingers inside of me.

The sensation is so much that I grip his hair and want to pull him from me, but I let go of him and claw at the wall as he continues.

"I can't...," I whimper as another near painful orgasm begins to build, but he doesn't stop until I am screaming and trembling on his thighs.

"Good girl," he groans against my center before pulling back from me, "You took that so well."

Holding me against the wall, he removes me from his shoulders and stands, immediately lifting my legs around his waist and turning off the water. Holding tight to my nearly limp body, he carries me out of the bathroom and lays me onto the bed while sliding himself inside of me.

Holding my thighs in his forearms, he stands at the edge of the bed and thrusts into me so hard I can barely breath. My back is arched off the bed and my clit is throbbing as he continues to punish me with orgasms.

"One more, *cuore mio,*" he groans as he leans down and pulls both our bodies further onto the bed, "It's going to come fast and hard while I fill you with my cum.

His hips pound into mine and the orgasm tears through me, my whole body is trembling as I scream out his name while he moans into my ear and empties himself inside of me.

Chapter Twenty-Nine

VENECIA

Every muscle in my body is sore when I try to stand from the bed.

"Careful, *cuore mio*," Dante reaches for me, "after that you might want to lay here a little while longer.

"After that, I'm pretty sure this whole fucking house knows that you are feeling better," I stand and realize just how unsteady my legs are, "we probably need to actually head downstairs."

"Along with having just survived torture, you want me to face your family after I just fucked you so hard you can barely walk?"

"Sir," I toss a t-shirt and pair of sweatpants at his naked body on the bed, "that second part you did to yourself. Now get up."

"Don't pretend you were an innocent party in all of this," he groans through his soreness as he slowly sits up on the edge of the bed. Grabbing my hand and pulling me between his legs, he wraps his arms around my waist and kisses my stomach before smiling up at me, "I love you, *cuore mio*."

"I love you too."

Releasing me he stretches for his clothes and pulls the shirt over his head before standing and putting on his pants.

Grabbing a pair of leggings and a shirt from my dresser, I quickly get dressed before brushing my wet hair and pulling it into a bun.

Standing at the door, I hesitate before reaching for the knob, nervous as to how everything is going to play out between Dante and the rest of my family.

"Go ahead," he says quietly from behind me, "I'm good."

Turning the knob, I step into the hallway and slowly walk down the stairs with Dante. Reaching the bottom, I can hear the majority of my family in the study. Dante's hand reaches for mine and our fingers lace together as we head down the hallway.

"Glad to hear," Ava pretends to stumble over her words with a stumble, "I mean see that you are feeling better."

"Jesus Christ, Avalie," I watch as Papa's cheeks redden with embarrassment for the first time in my life, "Is this the kind of shit I'm going to have to deal with now? It was bad enough knowing it was happening, we have to fucking talk about it too?"

"Sorry Papa," I glance at him, "we didn't mean-."

"What part of do we have to fucking talk about it does everyone not understand?"

Ava snickers at me as Papa fidgets in his seat. His current demeanor is like nothing I have ever seen – he is uncomfortable, embarrassed, and doesn't know how to react to this situation.

The discomfort in the room increases ten-fold as Renzo walks into the room.

He looks at Dante and his brows furrow.

DANTE

"Fuck," Lorenzo mumbles, "I'm assuming my sister didn't do that to your face."

"Renzo," Ava huffs at him.

"Sorry," he stumbles over his words, "I don't do this. Generally, when I beat the piss out of someone or torture the fuck out them, they're dead. So, I don't have to apologize."

"I heard V screaming while I was out for a run," he shifts uncomfortably, "and when I stumbled upon the two of you, I naturally assumed the worst. Forgive me, I didn't realize that the two of you were together. And it definitely didn't dawn on me that my baby sister would be into being playing out rape fantasies in the woods."

"Jesus fucking Christ, Renzo," Sal shifts in his chair with a bright red face.

"In all seriousness," Lorenzo walks towards me, "I'm sorry. I hope that someday we can manage to put this behind us."

"Things might be weird for a while, but we're good," I reach out to shake his hand, "She's lucky to have a family that loves and cares about her like all of you do."

Renzo takes a seat next to Ava, and I turn my attention to Sal.

"Sir?"

"Have a seat, son," he gestures for me to take a seat next to Venecia and she squeezes my hand as he talks, "I'm still fucking angry. But it was going to be someone eventually, and I'm happy it's you. Happy it's someone who would give their life for her like the rest of this of family would."

Standing from his seat to refill his drink, he puts his hand on my shoulder as he walks past me, "And it's not like I have any other daughters I have to worry about you knocking up."

"Jesus, Papa," Venecia huffs at him and the room fills with laughter.

Chapter Thirty

VENECIA

"Carlo," I squeal running down the front steps.

He left a few days after I got home. He and Marco have been working with the Armenians for months trying to track down Karyan.

Apparently one of Papa's contacts in Portugal had found her. By the time they got there to bring her back home, for both our family and Armenians to determine exactly how we wanted to deal with her, she was gone. Continuing to track her, they traveled to Italy, Panama and Japan before completely losing her. With no more leads, they are finally returning home.

Being so close in age, we've always been ridiculously close. This is probably the longest I've ever gone without seeing him. Taking me into his arms, he lifts me as he gently hugs me.

"V," he sets me down and looks me over, "it's time someone says something to you. You're getting fat."

"Fucking asshole," I swat at his arm, smacking him.

"I'm kidding," his hand rubs over the bump that is beginning to grow, "You look absolutely beautiful as usual. Pregnancy suits you."

Marco walks past us and his hand slides across Carlo's back, "We'll talk more later tonight."

"Um," I gesture at Marco and back to Carlo, "What the fuck was that?"

"It's nothing," he stutters back at me, "Just finishing stuff from our trip."

"Bull-fucking-shit," I snap back at him, "That's not nothing."

"It's nothing V."

"Hey," I gently nudge his chest, "Since when do we keep stuff from each other?"

"It probably started about the time you were fucking your hot, older bodyguard in secret," he grins quite obviously pleased with himself, "But it's nothing. Really, just tying up some stuff from our trip."

I'm about to call bullshit again, when Dante walks outside, giving Carlo an easy out of our current conversation.

"So," Carlo walks slowly towards Dante, "You're the one?"

"Yes," Dante begins to crack a small smile.

"You're the one that fucking knocked up my little sister," he swings a hard right hook into Dante's jaw knocking him to the ground.

Dante scrambles back to his feet, ready to beat the shit out of Carlo.

"What the fuck, Carlo," I yell as I race to get between the two of them.

Carlo puts out his hand towards Dante, "No hard feelings? I didn't want you to be the only guy to lay a hand on my sister that I didn't punch in the face. Since I heard my brother already broke your nose, I went easy on you."

"Your family is fucking crazy, *cuore mio*," Dante looks at me as he dusts himself off.

"You better get used to it," I smile at him, "they're all going to be your family soon enough.

"Excuse me," Carlo spins around to look at me, only to find me holding up my left hand to show him my engagement ring.

"Next month," I smirk at him and sarcastically continue, "I'm hoping to be able to walk down the aisle before I'm too fat for a decent wedding dress.

DANTE

"Congratulations," Carlo walks towards me and hugs me.

Pretty sure I'm never going to get used to the emotional swings of these Botticellis.

"Thanks," I hug him back.

"I got distracted when you took a swing at me," I pull back from our embrace, "your father asked me to hurry up and get you inside for a phone call with Dmitriy Andreyev."

"For the what?" his face scrunches in confusion.

"I don't know," I shrug back at him, "I'm just the messenger."

As Carlo heads inside, I walk towards Venecia and pull her against me. Gripping her face with both hands, I pull her mouth up to mine and kiss her deep until she is purring in my mouth.

"I was actually on my way out here to see you," I slide my hand into hers, "The contractor called. He has some question about the nursery he wants to discuss."

About two months ago, Sal started three construction projects on the estate property – a small home for each of his children. He keeps saying he started the project because Venecia, Carlo, and Lorenzo aren't kids anymore and they all need their own space. But being that he still doesn't quite trust these peace treaties with the other families, it's easier to keep everyone on the grounds with the same guards. With how close they all are as a family, if we all moved apart, I'm pretty sure we'd be traveling here daily anyway.

Sal doesn't seem to find it funny, but I'm quite certain he started the construction because he's tired of listening to Venecia and Avalie screaming at all hours of the night.

Based on the noises I heard coming from down the hall last night, I'm pretty sure I'm right.

Walking down the driveway, we turn down the newly poured driveway that occupies what used to be our morning running trail. With our fingers laced, we walk towards our home in mid-construction.

The fact that our house is being built in the same place Lorenzo had caught us in the woods, I've decided that Sal is a cheeky bastard with a sick fucking sense of humor.

Chapter Thirty-One

VENECIA

"V," Ava sighs at me, "It's not going to happen."

"It has to!"

"I'm trying," she groans, "but I don't think I can do it."

"Ava," I turn to face her, "I don't mean to be a bridezilla, but I don't care if you have to fucking sew me into this dress like it's Olivia Newton-John's pants in *Grease*, I am wearing this dress to walk down the aisle.

"Suck it in," she yanks hard on the dress, "and breathe out."

Doing as she asks, I feel the zipper slide up my back.

"Fuck...," I groan.

"Problem solved," she smiles back at me, "it's on.

"I was saying 'fuck' because it's tight as hell."

After helping me slide on my shoes, she begins walking me towards the ceremony at Papa's house on the compound.

"Not to pry," I squeeze her hand, "but I've got to talk to keep my mind off how fucking tight this dress is and weddings are the only thing on my mind right now."

"Me and Renzo?"

"Well, yeah."

"We aren't having one. As far as I'm concerned, we've been married since the same night you came home," she pulls the strap of her dress to the side exposing initials carved into her chest.

"Oh," I stammer at what to say, "That's, um, sweet."

She laughs at my response, "No. It's fucking crazy. But so are the two of us."

"I'm sorry for prying..."

"No you're not," she squeezes my hand, "You're my family, it's not prying. You are also taking my mind off things. I hadn't really thought about it until today, but the heads of both the Yakuza and the Armenians are going to be here today."

"Oh shit," I gasp, "Had I thought about that, I would've fucking eloped."

"It's okay," Ava smiles back at me, "Renzo and Sal spoke with my father. They both made it quite clear that if he attempts to force contact with me while he is here that it will be the end of the truce between the families."

"Venecia! Princess," Papa exclaims when he sees us approaching, "You look absolutely breathtaking."

"No time for sweet talk. I've got thirty minutes max before the constriction of this dress starts affecting your grandson."

Laughing, he takes my hand and we begin walking together.

DANTE

Standing at the altar, Renzo and Carlo stand behind me – my best men and my new brothers.

Weird to think that one of them was ready to kill me only a few months ago.

The small string ensemble begins playing, all the guests stand, and turn to look behind them. As the music plays, Sal walks Venecia down the aisle.

She is the most beautiful fucking thing I have ever seen in my life.

Standing before our family and friends, we proclaim what we have both known since we met. It was inevitable because we belong to each other.

"You may now kiss the bride..."

My lips crash into hers and I kiss my wife for the first time, before racing her back down the aisle. While Sal is throwing a little celebration in our honor, our guests believe we have left quickly for our honeymoon.

Instead, we are retreating to spend our first night in our newly finished home. Approaching the front door, I lift her into my arms and carry her over the threshold. Kicking the door shut with my foot, I carry her to straight upstairs to our master suite.

Carrying her to the bed, I sit her on the edge and kneel before her to remove her shoes, taking a moment to gently rub and kiss the soles of each of her feet.

Lifting the dress and kissing up her legs, I slowly stand before her and shed my tuxedo jacket.

"I think it's time we get you out of that dress, *cuore mio*, because I want to properly fuck my wife."

Standing her from the bed, I spin her around and slowly slide the zipper revealing her bare skin under the dress.

Chapter Thirty-Two

VENECIA

Grabbing the straps of the bodice, he slides them over my shoulders. The dress falls to my feet, leaving me standing before him in nothing but a sheer white thong.

He steps close behind me and I feel his lips slowly trail wet kisses down my spine as he kneels behind me. His fingers hook under the strings of my panties, and he slowly slides them down my legs.

I let out a small yelp when I feel his teeth sink into the flesh of my ass cheek, followed by a gentle slap as he stands. Dante unbuttons his shirt as he walks towards the nightstand. Sliding open the drawer, he pulls out a thin black scarf.

"Turn around," his voice deep as he walks back towards me.

He positions the scarf over my eyes, and I feel him tight it tightly, blindfolding me.

"On the bed," holding my hand he guides me to the edge and I climb onto it, "hands and knees."

Goosebumps prickle on my skin as I hear him undressing behind me.

"You know what it's like to watch yourself come," he startles me as his hands slowly slide over my hips and up my back, "now you learn what it's like to come when you are unable to anticipate what is going to happen to your body."

I can hear him rustling in the wooden drawer, and curiosity has me dying to know what he is doing and what he has planned for me.

"Based on your soaking wet cunt," a small whimper comes from my throat as I feel his finger slide through my slit, "I think you're going to like it."

His fingers slowly rub over and around my clit, both pleasuring me and teasing me at the same time. My hips flex against his fingers trying to get more.

"So greedy," he swirls them over my clit and I feel the mattress dip next to my body before his hands grab my hips and pull me back towards the edge of the bed, "Knees apart."

Spreading my knees further apart, his fingers return to my clit eliciting a string of airy whimpers as he works my body towards an orgasm. Just as I am approaching my release, his free hand squeezes my breast and rolls my nipple until I come.

Just as I am about to come down, I feel his tongue replacing his fingers on my clit. He is slow and teasing with the tip, torturing me by barely grazing over the bundle of nerves. He teases me for what feels like hours. My lips are trembling, and my clit is aching for him to let me come.

"Please," I moan against mattress, "Dante, please."

His tongue dives deep into my slit with firm, full strokes and I ride out my orgasm pressing back against him. As I am about to come down, he makes one slow, firm lick from my clit to my ass.

"If I remember correctly," he swirls his tongue around the hole, "you like my tongue back here."

"Mmmhmmm," the only response I am able to muster as he spreads my cheeks and presses his face between them before adding a thumb to my clit.

DANTE

Circling my tongue around her tight hole and rubbing my thumb over her clit, she is so fucking aroused that I can feel her pussy dripping on me. Continuing to work my tongue between her cheeks, quiet cries repeatedly rise from her chest.

"Do you need more?"

"Yes, please," she whimpers back to me.

Standing behind her, I grab the metal plug from the bed and coat it with lube before pressing it against her hole.

"This is to help get you ready for me," I push the tip inside of her before stopping to let her adjust to the sensation. She slowly pushes back towards me trying to take it deeper, and I slowly push the plug inside of her until the jewel is seated between her cheeks.

"So fucking beautiful," I growl at her, positioning the head of my cock against her entrance, "Can you take my cock in your tight little cunt with a plug in a your ass?"

"Yes," she groans against the sheets, her legs already beginning tremble.

In one solid stroke, I slide my length into her until I am buried to the hilt. Playing with the jewel in her ass, I slide myself in and out of her. She is so fucking tight with the plug filling her. Picking up speed, I continue to play with the plug causing her to moan and quiver beneath me. Reaching around, I rub over her clit and she clenches hard around my cock, biting the sheets and screaming as she comes hard.

Pressing my length deep inside of her, her back arches and I hold my hips still. With her cunt full of my cock, I pull on the plug, nearly removing it before pressing it back inside of her. Her hands are clawing at the sheets as I continue the motion, and I am ready to explode simply watching this plug stretch out her tight little hole.

A raspy sigh rumbles from her when I pull the plug from her, followed by a disappointed moan when I pull my cock from her as well.

Grabbing the lube, I thoroughly spread it over my already slick cock before putting my tip against the loosened hole of her ass. Holding the base, I slowly stretch her more until the head of my cock slides inside of her.

"You're doing so good," I continue to slowly slide inside of her, "taking my huge cock in your tight little ass."

Going slow, giving her time to adjust and ensure I don't hurt her, I slowly begin rocking my hips gently sliding in and out of her. Her breaths are fast and shallow, as she moans in rhythm with my thrusts.

"You're being such a good girl for me," I reach for her hands, "You fucking love the feel of me deep in your ass, don't you?"

"Yes," she cries back as I place her hands on her ass, prompting her to spread her cheeks for me, and she does.

Grabbing her wrists, I increase the speed and depth of my thrusts while watching my cock slide in and out of her hole.

"I'm going to need you to come for me, *cuore mio*," I reach my hand around her hips and rub over her clit. Her whole body shakes as she comes, her tight hole squeezing tightly around my cock. An animalistic roar rattles from my chest, my cock quivering and throbbing inside of her as I fill her with my cum.

Slowly pulling out of her, I climb onto the bed and pull her fatigued body into my arms before removing the blindfold and claiming her mouth with my tongue.

"I love you, *mia moglie*. Always, *cuore mio*."

Chapter Thirty-Three

VENECIA

Happy birthday, dear Tony. Happy birthday to you...

Our family is gathered around the dining room table. Looking across the table at Papa, Avalie, Renzo, Luca, Carlo, Irena, Dmitryi and Marco, I cannot help but smile as the scariest members of the most ruthless crime syndicate on the East Coast sing *Happy Birthday* to a two-year-old while wearing ridiculous cardboard party hats.

What might be considered normal for most families is definitely not normal for mine.

After blowing out candles, eating significantly more sugary cake than any two-year old needs, and running through the yard most of the afternoon, Tony is in dire need of a nap.

"I got him," Renzo scoops him from the ground to carry him upstairs.

Tony squirms in his arms, struggling to get down while screaming, "No. No, Unca Renzo. PopPop take me."

"Hand my future mafia kingpin over," Papa extends his arms, "I'll take him."

"Papa," I sigh, "How many times have I told you to stop calling him that?"

Watching Tony giggle as Papa carries him into the house, a smile spreads over my face. It only grows when I feel Dante step behind me and slide his hands around me.

"Have you thought about what you want to name her?" he rubs his hands over my swollen belly.

Placing my hands on top of his, together hold we hold our little girl growing my belly.

"I want to name her Amelia," I tilt my face up to him.

"I think your mom would be honored to be the namesake of her first granddaughter," he smiles back down at me before kissing my forehead.

"Maybe you should go lay down too, *cuore mio*," his hands continue to rub over my stomach, "I know you must be exhausted."

"I'm not *that* tired," I lean against him, "but I could go lay down. Everyone is heading home, and Papa will have Tony napping at his house for at least the next two hours."

"I guess we're about to find out how many times in two hours I can make that sweet little cunt come on my tongue and around my cock."

Thank You For Reading

I hope you enjoyed Dante and Venecia's story!

If you did, the best support you can give to an indie author, like myself, is to tell others about my book. Reviews left on Goodreads, Amazon, or anywhere else you are comfortable truly mean the world to me.

* * *

Dante and Venecia's story are part of an interconnected, stand-alone series. Want to know about what started the chaos? Check out her brother Lorenzo's story *Sold To The Syndicate*.

Next up in this series is the story of Giancarlo, Venicea's other brother, in *Indebted To The Enemy*.

Also by JL Quick

SOLD TO THE SYNDICATE: THE BOTTICELLI BROTHERHOOD SERIES

Lorenzo Botticelli is like royalty. His family runs this city. He is brutal, ruthless and always in control. He is not a man to be messed with.

Avalie is a sassy, sarcastic woman who has spent her life learning how to fend for herself. She is not the type of woman you control.

Lorenzo owns her now, sold to him to pay a debt. Avalie quickly shows him that she is not going to roll over and play nice as a hostage.

A steamy battle of wills ensues as they fight to determine which of them will break first. Will it be her? Or will it be him?

IGNITE THE FIRE: BURNING FIRE BOOK ONE

Most kids grow up afraid of the monsters under their bed. Not me. I grew up terrified of the one that crawled into mine.

As an adult that same monster still haunts my dreams. My nightmares.

The monster has ruined me and taken away my ability to be touched.

Until him. We met in passing, by pure chance, one night.

His touch is the first that doesn't repulse me. His touch makes me feel alive. And it's terrifying.

SCORCHED EARTH: BURNING FIRE BOOK TWO

The love of Liam's life, the first person he ever truly cared about, has been taken from him.

Hunting down the monster that took her from his life is personal, and he is determined to ensure they pay.

Made in the USA
Middletown, DE
24 June 2023